1395

808.3874 Braun.M

Braun, Matthew.

How to write western novels

OCT 3 1 1988

How to Write Western Novels

HOW TO WRITE WESTERN NOVELS

by
Matt Braun

EVANSTON PUBLIC LIBRARY
1703 ORRINGTON AVENUE
EVANSTON, ILLINOIS 60201

Writer's Digest Books

Cincinnati, Ohio

How to Write Western Novels.
Copyright © 1988 by Matt Braun. Printed
and bound in the United States of America. All rights reserved. No part of this
book may be reproduced in any form or
by any electronic or mechanical means including information storage and retrieval
systems without permission in writing
from the publisher, except by a reviewer,
who may quote brief passages in a review.
Published by Writer's Digest Books, an
imprint of F&W Publications, Inc., 1507
Dana Ave., Cincinnati, Ohio 45207. First
edition.

93 92 91 90 89 88   5 4 3 2 1

**Library of Congress Cataloging-
in-Publication Data**

Braun, Matthew.
  How to write western novels/by Matt
Braun.—1st ed.
    p. cm.
  Includes index.
  ISBN 0-89879-321-1: $11.95
    1. Western stories—Authorship. I. Title.
PN3377.5.W47B74 1988   88-10824
808.3′874—dc19   CIP

Design by Carol Buchanan

The following page constitutes an extension of this copyright page.

To:

Bettiane

Who saw beyond the rough edges

Contents

Permissions

Material excerpted from *The Big Sky* copyright © 1972 by A.B. Guthrie, Jr. reprinted by permission of the author.

Material excerpted from *A Conspiracy of Knaves* copyright © 1987 by Dee Brown reprinted by permission of the author.

Material excerpted from *The Good Old Boys* copyright © 1987 by Elmer Kelton reprinted by permission of the author.

Introduction
A Craftsman on His Trade

Mark Twain was fond of telling a story about the process by which boys mature into men. To paraphrase the old curmudgeon, he said: "At sixteen I believed my father to be one of the most ignorant men in the world. At twenty-one I was amazed to see how smart he'd become in only five short years."

Perhaps the story is apocryphal. But it nonetheless strikes a parallel with the way in which writers mature at their trade. Certainly it typifies how I finally wised up to what the craft of writing is all about. The path I took might be characterized as the long-way-round.

All my life I wanted to be a writer. In particular, I wanted to write novels dealing with the Old West. Heritage provided the motivation, for my roots span several generations of Westerners. On one side of the family, my great-grandfather established a ranch in Oklahoma. On the other side, a number of my ancestors were members of the Cherokee tribe. It seemed only natural that I would one day tell stories of a bygone time.

That day finally rolled around. In 1969, at age thirty-six, I decided it was "now or never." I sold everything I owned and quit my job. A week later I moved into a cabin located in a remote stretch of mountains. While I had worked as a journalist, I had no formal training in writing fiction. Nor had I ever read a book on the craft of writing. What I had instead was determination and a degree of rough talent. I gave myself a year to write a salable Western novel.

Three years later I was still an "unpublished author." I had written four novels, none of which had found a publisher. Hard at work on the fifth novel, I was convinced my writing showed improvement with each effort. Odd jobs kept food on the table and I continued to hammer away at the typewriter. Then, within a period of ten days, my agent sold the fourth and fifth novels. The latter was purchased on the basis of a half-completed manuscript.

There's nothing extraordinary in my personal story. Lots of writers have endured hard times along the road to being published. Yet there's a tale to be told in what happened afterward. In some ways it's a precautionary tale, for it happens to many greenhorn writers. The central point, however, relates to the way a writer matures at his trade. Some learn faster than others.

When I began writing in 1969, I was all too aware that I knew nothing about crafting a novel. By 1973, when I'd had four novels published, I was convinced that I knew virtually all there was to know about writing. The belief was strengthened by the fact that no editor had ever asked for revisions on any of the books.

By 1974, with six books published, I had convinced myself that I was the Faulkner of the Western novel. I saw my work as literature—literature in the sense that it was art. Some Western writers will recall I wrote articles drawing unfavorable comparisons between traditional Westerns and literature. To put it charitably, I took myself very seriously indeed.

Then I got lucky. In 1975, I found a mentor by the name of Jerrold Mundis. A superb writer, Mundis has received critical acclaim for his works of literature. Under a pseudonym, he has also realized considerable success in writing commercial novels. Mundis did me the great favor of editing every sentence of two books, after they had been published. Once you've seen your work—in book form—treated to the red pencil, you learn the true meaning of angst. It was a humbling experience.

By the end of 1975, I realized I was not all that brilliant a writer. Even though I'd had eight novels published at that point, it became apparent that I had a good deal to learn about my craft. In effect, Mundis had employed a variation of shock treatment, and it worked. I was receptive, at last, to a long overdue message.

With my mentor's guidance, I undertook a program of self-instruction. I began an omnivorous reading course: classics, historical novels, mysteries and spy thrillers, and bestsellers. Many of these works, particularly those on the bestseller list, I had previously dismissed as commercial trash. Discovery followed discovery, and there was a gradual dawning that "literature" was not my strong suit. What I enjoyed reading most—and writing—was a romping good story.

I ultimately arrived at a set of guidelines that turned me around as a writer. There's nothing new or profound in these guidelines, and I suspect that every successful writer follows something similar. But what I've taken as my personal yardstick illustrates how a writer matures by getting back to the basics of his craft.

There are five guidelines in total. Throughout this book, I will cover three of them at considerable length. To simply list them here would dilute their critical nature, for they represent a summation of the rules of good writing. The fourth guideline requires no great elaboration. While specific, it's nonetheless a personal statement. A belief I know now to be true. A hard fact of our trade.

Art is for painters and literature is a plateau achieved by perhaps one in a thousand writers. The journeyman writer—the craftsman—must strive to engage the reader with a solid story. Having achieved that with regularity, he can then aspire to one day writing the great American novel. Personally, I've reconciled myself to the fact that I will never write a literary classic. I'm content instead to write a damn good Western.

Suffice it to say I've lived by these guidelines. With each passing year—from 1975 on—I became ever more conscious of how little I knew about the craft of writing. Of greater significance, I realized that no one ever truly *masters* the craft. We are instead lifelong students of an intricate process that defies absolute comprehension.

Somewhere along this road of enlightenment, I began to see myself in a more realistic vein. I discovered I was a craftsman, not an artist and never a literary oracle. In a word, I was a storyteller, and like storytellers throughout the ages, my one imperative was to cast a spell with words. To capture the reader's interest, to occasionally entrance him, and above all else, to entertain him.

All of which brings me to the fifth and final guideline that I've adopted for myself. A good story, even when it's told with modest talent, will be read and remembered. A bad story, even when it's told with brilliance, will be appreciated by no one but literary pretenders. In the final analysis, the craftsman knows that it's 90 percent sweat and 10 percent inspiration. He labors to write a good story, and having done so, he takes justifiable pride in his effort.

All writers, of course, strive to improve with each new book. To date, I have written thirty-one novels and three nonfiction works. Since 1975, when I came under the tutelage of Jerrold Mundis, I believe my books have shown marked improvement. Granted, the statement is somewhat subjective; but writers I respect are in complete agreement. Like myself, I hasten to add, they are all craftsmen, solid storytellers. Not an artist in the bunch.

The literary establishment will never shower me with accolades. But then, I long ago cast aside the pretense of writing literature. So the indifference of the literati merits nothing more than a large ho hum. I write these days for the readers, rather than the artsy-smartsy community. Which is not to say I wouldn't like the prestige and recognition that comes with a Pulitzer. From a pragmatic standpoint, however, I'm not holding my breath.

A story will serve to illustrate the point. In 1985, I journeyed to New Mexico for research on two novels. One item on my list was to "walk" the headquarters site of John Chisum's Jinglebob Ranch. Through various helpful people, I discovered that it was still a working outfit and finally found myself face-to-face with the foreman. We talked for a while and he agreed to arrange a tour of the original site. At that point, I had identified myself only by name, commenting that I was researching a book. Abruptly, he stopped and subjected me to a long, searching stare. Then a sudden light of recognition crossed his features.

"Matt Braun!" He beamed. "Gawddamn, I read your books!"

I won't forget the look on his face. Nor will I forget how he remembered titles and various characters from my books. Listening to him, I was reminded once again of what counts most. Awards and literary recognition are strictly second place.

First prize for a storyteller can be reduced to a simple, declarative sentence. *Gawddamn, I read your books!*

1.
The Western

The marvelous thing about the Western genre is that it accommodates virtually every category of fiction. Adventure, mystery, romance, and historical saga are all easily adapted to a Western format. In fact, some or all of these elements can be combined within the same novel.

Several writers have selected the Western frontier as the setting for romance novels played out against an historic backdrop. Others have put together a blend of romance and historical saga, the love story being the focal point. Any number of novels have been constructed around the Pinkerton Detective Agency, combining mystery and adventure in one package. There are also contemporary mysteries which owe much of their success to a Western setting. Clearly, the variations possible within the genre are limited only by your imagination.

Some writers hopscotch from genre to genre. They write a Western, then a mystery, and follow it with a steamy romance. These jacks-of-all-trades are competent writers and usually earn an excellent livelihood. One writer I know has achieved remarkable success in both mysteries and Westerns. On occasion, I myself have dabbled in the field of contemporary occult novels. However, these excursions into foreign terrain were prompted by story ideas too compelling to set aside. Once the novels were written, I immediately returned to my chosen field. I suspect most Western writers stick with the genre for reasons similar to my own. Nothing of the modern world equals the wonder of a wide-open frontier. There was never anything like it!

For much of the 19th Century, vast distances separated the civilized East and the wilderness West. Enterprising writers, pandering to the romantic notions of the reading public, transformed fact into fantasy until the West became an exotic and mystical land, a place of myth. Thus, in a relatively short period of time, the Western man became a part of our folklore, the central figure in our national mythology.

Dime novels of the era employed sensationalism and lurid writing to depict the heroics associated with the frontier. Erastus Beadle, of the Beadle and Adams publishing company, issued the first dime novel in 1860. His goal was the mass distribution of fiction, evoking themes that would appeal to a mass audience. The wild and woolly West, distant from the niceties of a structured society, became the setting of the dime novels.

Over a period of thirty years various publishers churned out more than thirty Western series. Dime novels were immensely popular with the Eastern public, and some of the series had as many as three hundred titles. Kit Carson, Buffalo Bill Cody, and Wild Bill Hickok, performing fictional feats of heroism, were shortly enshrined in the pantheon of Western folklore. The purpose of the dime novel was not to portray the West accurately, but to provide the adventure and sensationalism expected by the readers. The formulaic characters and plots were a commercial virtue since the public wanted a mythical West, romantic and larger than life.

The cowboy rode to prominence in dime novels in the late 1880s. No mere herder of cattle, he was depicted as a gunman fighting outlaws and Indians. The romantic vision of the Wild West was thus a world more real in imagination than in fact. The first pulp magazines, which appeared in the 1890s, were merely slicker versions of the dime novels. Owen Wister's *The Virginian* was a full-fledged novel, and ultimately sold more than a million copies. Published in 1902, it further established the cowboy as an icon of the Old West. Wister was generally credited with originating the "formula Western" novel, wherein good battled evil and gallantry typified manliness.

The formula Western became a staple for writers like Zane Grey, an Eastern dentist turned novelist, and the prolific Max Brand. Grey's *Riders of the Purple Sage*, published in 1912, remains the most widely known Western of all time. The influence of Brand and Grey, and a later writer, Ernest Haycox, proved to be profound. Their work is a direct link to the novels of more contemporary writers, men such as Louis L'Amour and Luke Short. Serious students of the genre have always debated the merits of the formula Western. Yet no one denies that it has sold millions upon millions of books.

Other novelists have depicted the Old West in more literal terms, stripped of its myth. Among the better known are writers such as A. B. Guthrie, Vardis Fisher, and Frederick Manfred. Their work is generally considered literature, and as a result, none of them has developed the mass following of formula writers. Nonetheless, their novels illustrate how the genre has evolved in slightly more than a hundred years. From pulp-school potboiler to classic literature, there is something for everyone in the Western field.

The Mythical West

Of course, a fledgling writer should never lose sight of the symbolic nature of Westerns. Any novel set in the Old West, whatever its literary merits, represents a legendary time in our national consciousness. In the 1860s, the United States was not yet a hundred years old. America had no mythology of its own, no fabled characters such as Beowulf and Roland. So we invented a cast of mythical creatures, the cowboys and gunfighters and plainsmen of the Western frontier. We combined the King Arthur legends with the medieval morality plays, adding the chivalric code of the Old West into the mix, and called it a Western. All in a matter of years, we created the literature of our newly invented mythology.

Nowhere in history have mythical figures achieved such widespread appeal. Few people today would recall that Beowulf met a valorous death while slaying the evil dragon. But people around the world, from Germany to Japan, can relate the story of Wyatt Earp and the Gunfight at the O.K. Corral. Who cares if Wyatt Earp wasn't all that chivalrous and the gunfight itself was something less than good versus evil? The myth of the Old West encompasses knaves and rascals as well as stalwart knights attired in buckskins. Nothing before or since has so captured the imagination of a global audience. The Old West endures as a place of legend, a time of legendary feats.

A writer of Westerns must keep the myth uppermost in mind. Whether he writes high literature or ordinary shoot-'em-ups, the mythology of that time and place is omnipresent. To some degree, an historical novelist can separate truth from fancy. Still, however accurate his work, his perception of the Old West stems in part from the mythology. Even more significant, the reading public will not be denied its legends. No writer, if he's honest with himself, would disclaim the mythical origins of his work. In the end, all Western writers write of a fabled land, and legends.

Let's presume you've decided to become a Western writer. If you're like most writers, you were obsessed with the notion long before you made the decision. Your hesitation lay in not knowing what you wanted to write. So perhaps it's time to ask yourself what sort of Western you really like. As a general rule, you'll write best what you most enjoy reading. That's no small consideration in planning a novel.

To the extent that a novel follows the stereotypical formula, it is a commercial endeavor. To the extent that a novel is original in concept, and transcends the formula, it assumes some degree of distinction. There is clearly every shade of literary merit, from none to exemplary, in fiction of the West. The Western Writers of America included two of A. B. Guthrie's novels in a list of all-time "Best Westerns." Yet he was also awarded the Pulitzer Prize for literature. Perhaps, as in other schools of writing, some Western craftsmen are simply better at their trade.

Future of the Western

The market for Western fiction is currently very strong. Less than ten years ago, however, publishers declared the Western novel moribund. Paperback houses curtailed production drastically, and many limited their Western line to the reissue of old books. Those that remained active in the field were, for the most part, the publishers of Adult Westerns.

The demise of Western movies and television series foreshadowed the decline of Western novels. America's long romance with cowboys and gunfighters seemed at an end. Upscale urbanites favored mysteries, science fiction, and mainstream bestsellers. The great heartland of America preferred gothic romances and adventure yarns to tales of the frontier. In an age of high technology, public and publishers alike looked upon the Western as an anachronism.

By 1985, however, something extraordinary happened. Several novels of the West, published as mainstream fiction, revitalized the interest in Westerns. Paperback houses began publishing traditional as well as historical genre novels. In the space of two years, a market once pronounced dead was suddenly brought to life. By no means were Westerns a national preoccupation, as in the 1950s. Yet Americans had not entirely lost interest in that mythical land of yesteryear. A crackling good tale, told with realism and authenticity, was once again back in vogue.

Today, every paperback house has an expanded line of Westerns. Editors are acquiring original works, and even appear receptive to the efforts of beginning writers. Hardcover houses continue to publish novels of the West as mainstream fiction, and many have shown renewed interest in both historical and traditional genre novels. The market is, in a word, flourishing.

Traditional Western

The Traditional Western can be defined as a novel dealing with the mythology of the Old West. Typically, it is 60,000-70,000 words in length and structured along a single story line. The length effectively precludes multiple subplots and the complexities encountered with a large cast of characters.

A classic example of the Traditional Western would be Jack Schaefer's *Shane*. The myths most familiar to readers are all present in the novel. There were ruthless cattle barons in the Old West. Some of those cattle barons, employing violent tactics, attempted to drive sodbusters off their homesteads. And the frontier also produced a breed of men who came to be known as gunfighters.

Myth supplants reality, however, when a gunfighter voluntarily appoints himself the champion of the beleaguered sodbusters. Quite the contrary, hired guns worked for the wealthy and the powerful, the ranchers and the cattlemen's associations. Just such a gunman was imported by the cattle baron in *Shane*. Drawn true to life, but still a mythical figure, he was properly portrayed as an assassin.

Schaefer masterfully added yet another element to the mix. His gunfighter, Shane, was a figure of mystery. There was the clear impression that Shane was trying to outdistance his past, hang up his guns. But the plight of the sodbusters evoked moral outrage, some sense of fair play. Like a paladin of medieval times, Shane rode to the rescue, armor and lance replaced by a six-gun. The feat was no less heroic, or mythical, than the deeds of Sir Galahad. Brilliantly crafted, *Shane* is a tale of what might have been. What we would like to believe actually happened on the frontier. In short, a Traditional Western.

Historical Western

By contrast, the Historical Western strives to recreate a measure of reality. These are typically large books, 90,000-150,000 words in length. The expansive nature of an Historical Western allows more than one story line, multiple subplots, and a large cast of characters. Some writers regularly use actual historical figures as primary characters in their novels. Other writers prefer to limit historical figures to a secondary role. Still another group recasts historical figures with fictional names and proceeds to structure stories around actual events. A certain literary license permits the writer to fictionalize the pages of history.

On the other hand, nothing permits a writer to rewrite history. To shift events in time, or place an historical figure where he never appeared, takes literary license beyond reasonable limits. The one exception would be a disclaimer by the writer, usually in the form of an Author's Note, to the effect that he has revised facts for the purpose of tightening the story. Even then, the writer has an obligation to portray people and events with a large degree of accuracy. To be effective, any Western novel must have an authentic flavor. An Historical Western must combine authenticity with accuracy, never straying far from the truth. The myth must somehow be cloaked in reality.

A. B. Guthrie's *The Big Sky* provides an excellent example of the Historical Western. While fictional in nature, the novel renders an accurate portrayal of the mountain men. Actual historical figures are relegated to secondary roles, appearing infrequently and only then when it enhances the plot. Their time onstage is limited and their actions are presented within the context of factual events. Guthrie employs literary license with a deft touch, and there's no attempt to rewrite history. His aim is to recreate an instant from that bygone time, when men in buckskins wandered an unmarked wilderness. He does it admirably.

The mythic aspects of the mountain men are woven into *The Big Sky*. Yet the protagonist, Boone Caudill, has more reality about him than myth. The story traces Caudill's passage from a greenhorn to a seasoned fur trapper, accurately portraying the life such men led. Guthrie writes of the mountains and plains with a lyric quality, creating a background to match the power of his story. The authentic flavor of the novel, which indicates massive research, plays a central role in the overall structure. The reader knows it's fiction based on fact; there's a ring of truth to everything that happens. *The Big Sky* achieves what all historical novels strive to attain. The place and the people come alive within a world that no longer exists. That instant in time assumes the mantle of reality.

Series Western

Western series novels are not limited to one format. Generally speaking, there are historical series and traditional series. However, the writer has great leeway, and lots of room for innovation. The first series I wrote was about a private detective in the Old West. Though a little-known fact, there were private detective agencies other than the Pinkertons operating in the West. I patterned my fictional detective on two such Western sleuths.

The cardinal rule for writing a series has to do with the principal character, or characters. To succeed, the lead character must be one who will hold the reader's interest through several novels. He should be unique but still mortal, slightly larger than life. Whatever trade he follows, he must exhibit a high degree of skill. Moreover, his physical characteristics and personal traits must be consistent throughout successive novels. Lastly, his name must command attention, set him apart.

The name I chose for my fictional detective was Luke Starbuck. He was the premier manhunter of his day, headquartered in Denver. His profession allowed him to roam the West, which fulfilled yet another fundamental of series novels. The emphasis should be on plot and action, and the locale should shift book by book across a broad spectrum of the frontier. By pegging the series around a detective, I was also able to bring onstage true-life outlaws such as Billy the Kid, Jesse James, and Butch Cassidy. Luke Starbuck performed admirably as a series character, ultimately extending to a total of eight books.

A traditional Western series is structured somewhat similarly. The protagonist is generally a nomadic loner who wanders the far corners of the West. The plots are diverse, sometimes loosely based on historical events, and each novel must be crafted to stand on its own. Of course, the pilot novel should establish the character of the protagonist and set the tone for the series. To a large extent, the first book determines whether readers will follow the lead character into future adventures. Here again, the emphasis is on action rather than any deep character study. Wherever the protagonist travels, trouble must shortly follow.

The historical series is somewhat more complex. To be effective, it must revolve around actual events and real characters. Fictional characters are created as a device to advance the story through time and place. These fictional characters also serve as the protagonists, and therein arises the complexity. Somewhat like a family saga, an historical series will usually cover two or more generations. Some characters die, others are born, and the writer is presented with the task of advancing the clock through a long span of years. All the while, the historical aspects of each novel must be portrayed accurately, which requires massive research. Writing an historical series can be compared to a juggling act in which the objects being juggled are periodically switched. Clearly, it's a challenge for even the most skilled writer.

The Brannocks was the first book in what I envisioned as a trilogy. Through the lives of three brothers, I intended to tell the story of the Westward Expansion. By the time I finished the second book, I realized the trilogy would have to be expanded. The scope of the story was simply too large, and the Brannocks kept producing more offspring. Compounding matters was an enormous cast of historical characters and a list of critically important historical events. The series spread outward from Colorado to Texas, Indian Territory, New Mexico, and points westward. In the end, the trilogy became four books, with a total length of almost half a million words. I stopped before the Brannocks had too many more babies. It might have gone on forever.

Writing series novels is not for everyone. Even the simplest of the lot, the traditional series format, requires long-range planning and a certain logistical genius. Still, for all the headaches entailed, it can be a rewarding experience. Luke Starbuck and the Brannock brothers were a source of great personal fulfillment. Western series novels can also be quite profitable.

Novels of the West

There is yet another category of Western, though it could hardly be labeled a subgenre. Instead, these books are mainstream novels with a Western setting, written by some of our finest authors. Their literary merit has expanded the definition of *Western* within the last few years.

In fact, these books are simply novels of the West. What distinguishes them is that they are crafted with excellence and strike a literary tone.

Originally published in hardcover, these books also draw the attention of major reviewers throughout the country. Some of them appear from time to time on one or more of the bestseller lists.

A partial roll call would include the following titles: *Lonesome Dove* by Larry McMurtry (Simon & Schuster), which won the Pulitzer Prize; *Deadwood* by Pete Dexter (Random House); *Lords of the Plain* by Max Crawford (Atheneum); *The Snowblind Moon* by John Byrne Cooke (Simon & Schuster); *Winterkill* by Craig Lesley (Houghton Mifflin); *Heart of the Country* by Greg Matthews (W. W. Norton); *The Blind Corral* by Ralph Robert Beer (Viking Press).

The list is by no means exhaustive. In recent years, virtually every hardcover publisher has proven receptive to novels of the West. The length of such books varies between 80,000 and 250,000 words. The excellence of plotting and characterization varies only by degree. These are mainstream novels, read by a mainstream audience, In that sense, it might be said that they transcend the genre.

Young Adult Western

A Young Adult Western, as the name implies, is written for an audience of ages ten to fifteen. These are short novels, rarely more than 30,000 words in length. Young adult books are widely reviewed, particularly for the library market. A writer who develops a following can do quite well within the subgenre.

The critical factor for the writer is that his story must somehow relate to today's youngsters. That means a firsthand knowledge of kids and what interests them most. Their tastes are not the same as adults, and the book should be tailored accordingly. No writer should embark on what amounts to a specialized field until he has developed insights into the younger generation.

All the rules of good plotting apply. A conflict should be established early on, with the characters struggling toward a resolution while undergoing assorted trials and tribulations. Young adults are usually more intrigued by problems evolving within themselves. One example is the almost universal belief by youngsters that they are misunderstood. Few young people feel truly appreciated, or respected, by adults.

Young readers tend to identify with characters who are somehow like themselves. Perhaps the character defies his parents, tells white lies, and plays hooky from school. Or perhaps he's a show-off, something of a prankster, and finds it difficult to conduct himself according to conventional behavior. Common problems are learning to accept responsibility, developing self-reliance, and overcoming mistakes in the face of adult criticism. The list could be expanded to encompass all the pitfalls associated with growing up.

Adventure, of course, must be interwoven with personal problems. A character might find himself involved with outlaws, or working as a nighthawk on a cattle drive. Perhaps his parents are killed, or abandon him, and he's forced to fend for himself. Such things happened in the Old West just as they happen in today's world. For the story to be plausible, however, the period must be meticulously researched. A writer should never shortchange his audience simply because they are young.

Nor should the writer overlook another important consideration. A great many young adult books feature a lead female character. There were at least as many girls in the Old West as there were boys. And their problems as well as their adventures were no less absorbing because of their gender. The point taken is that a Young Adult Western need not necessarily be written for boys. Girls also like a romping good story.

Western Short Story

The Western Short Story is virtually extinct. In years past, magazines devoted to Western short stories were as popular as those for mystery and science fiction. All such publications have now disappeared from the racks.

Why do people buy Western novels but not short stories? The reason most often voiced has to do with the quality of the material. For the most part, Western short stories were dominated by cardboard characters and clichéd plots. The readers finally got their fill of bad writing.

Which is not to say that all short stories were poorly done. Among others, Dorothy Johnson and Elmer Kelton proved that short stories could be crafted with great skill. In large measure, however, the short story was the domain of writers who simply hadn't mastered their trade. The demand gradually dwindled off to nothing.

Today, there is a limited market. Some literary magazines, such as *Triquarterly*, will occasionally accept Western short stories. I had one published in *Antaeus*, which advertises itself as "popular fiction." To some small degree, there is also renewed interest by publishers in Western anthologies. Yet the problem for the beginning writer remains much the same. Publishers will generally consider only established authors when putting together an anthology.

The future of the traditional Western Short Story appears tenuous. Instead, the trend will probably be toward contemporary stories of the modern West. There are compelling tales to be told of today's West, and some writers have already moved in that direction. Others are thinking in terms of the "crossover" reader, combining elements of various genres. One example would be a mystery short story with a modern Western setting. The best advice would be to explore the market, query magazine editors, and find out what's selling. A short story writer, more so than most, must be willing to adapt to changing conditions. Supply and demand dictate in a relatively narrow marketplace.

Adult Western

An Adult Western can be defined as a novel in which sex is the dominant theme. Some are merely risque. Others are so explicit as to be pornographic. Traditionalists, of course, believe such works have sullied the Western novel by dwelling on the overactive libido of the characters. There was nonetheless a strong market for such novels, and the demand grew rapidly. In the 1980s, Adult Westerns became the staple of many paperback houses.

For the most part, these books are written under "house names," or pseudonyms. The audience for such novels is not altogether the same readership as for traditional Westerns. One reason is that many Adult Westerns depict sadistic violence as well as kinky sex. In some of the books, there is an attempt to straddle the fence between adult and traditional. Traditional themes such as lawmen versus outlaws, and cattlemen versus sodbusters, are used as a fulcrum for steamy sex and gratuitous violence. The device is readily transparent to even casual readers.

The better known Adult Western series are owned by the publisher. Typically, a series will have two or more writers, all of them writing under the same pen name. As a result, consistency is not the strong suit of such books. The style of writing, not to mention character traits, will vary widely from book to book. For all their faults, however, Adult Westerns can be crafted with skill. A traditional story line, limited to perhaps two or three sex scenes, vastly improves the overall quality. Wanton violence should be ditched entirely.

The future of the Western has never looked brighter. The traditional attributes of the frontier—individualism and resourcefulness—are once more perceived as an essential part of our culture. The day when horse operas and shoot-'em-ups dominated the book racks has passed. But a novel with fully realized characters and good plotting stands an excellent chance of being published. American readers of today are intrigued by an authentic portrayal of our national mythology.

To succeed, a writer has only to depict it as it actually happened.

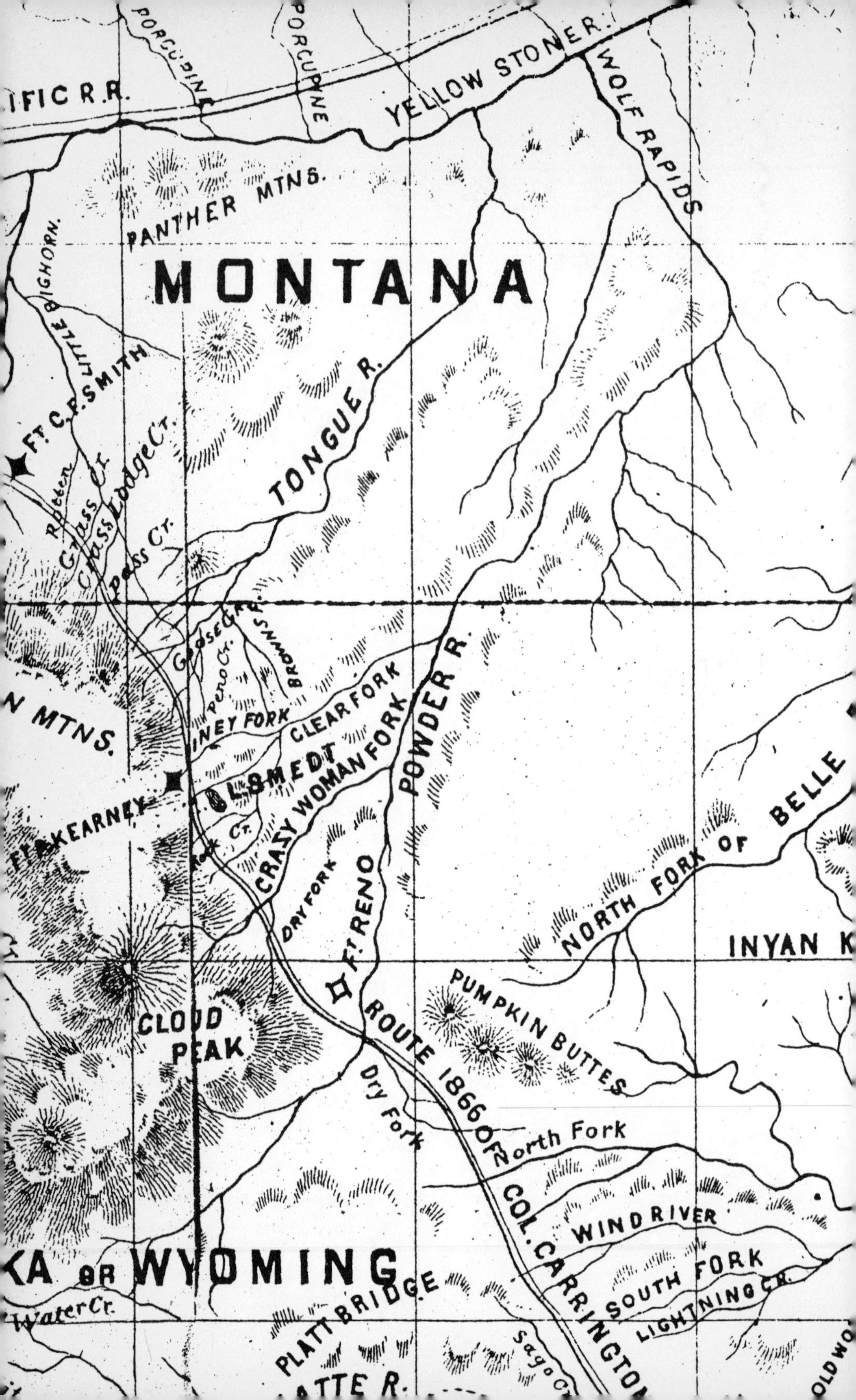

IFIC R.R.
PORCUPINE
PORCUPINE
YELLOW STONE R.
WOLF RAPIDS
PANTHER MTNS.
MONTANA
LITTLE BIGHORN.
Ft. C.F. SMITH
Rotten
Grass Cr.
Grass Lodge Cr.
Pass Cr.
TONGUE R.
Goose Cr.
Peno Cr.
BROWNS F.
INEY FORK
CLEAR FORK
N MTNS.
Ft. P. KEARNEY
Rock Cr.
CRASY WOMAN FORK
POWDER R.
DRY FORK
Ft. RENO
NORTH FORK OF BELLE
INYAN K
PUMPKIN BUTTES
CLOUD PEAK
ROUTE 1866 OF COL. CARRINGTON
Dry Fork
North Fork
WIND RIVER
SOUTH FORK
LIGHTNING CR.
KA OR WYOMING
Water Cr.
PLATT BRIDGE
Sago Cr.
ATTE R.
OLD WO

2.
From Concept
to Plot

he tale of the West is epic in dimension. Within fifty years, roughly 1840 to 1890, half a continent was won and settled. From that westward expansion of a nation emerged stories yet to be told. The truth of the frontier was vivid beyond the imaginings of any novelist, and within the reality of the West lies the seed of plot and theme.

If you aspire to write a credible Western you must first steep yourself in the lore of that bygone time. Your path will be threefold, a search for knowledge: (1) an obsession with the history of the Old West; (2) a passion for research and an eagerness to devour every nonfiction work written on the era; (3) an analytical study of the works of such novelists as Dee Brown, A. B. Guthrie, and Elmer Kelton. These writers are masters of characterization, plot, and theme, all rendered with authenticity and realism. Nothing could be more instructive than an in-depth scrutiny of their novels.

Keep in mind, plot is not some arcane subject restricted to great works of literature. Simply stated, plot represents events structured into a story line. Who does what, and when and how it happens. Formula Westerns, according to conventional wisdom, are limited to nine plots: The cavalry and Indians story, the repentant gunfighter story, the lawman story, the outlaw story, the railroad story, the ranch story, the range war story, the revenge story, and the rustler story.

Interestingly, many of the major works in the Western field have employed these same plots. Critics and scholars consider several of them to be classics, works of literature. So what separates a potboiler from a first-rate novel? When the same plot and theme are used, why does one writer stand apart from another? Talent alone isn't the answer.

The hack takes the easy way. He apes what's been done before and usually adds some flaws of his own. The writer who stands apart takes the risk of using a shopworn idea in a new way. He works a variation on plot, struggles to invent a twist on theme, and creates characters who are equal to his vision. In short, he strives for originality, something uniquely his own. And in that one word lies the answer. Originality separates mediocrity from excellence.

A source of excellence can be found in the novels of other Western writers. As you read for entertainment, analyze the work of writers you admire. Get down to the nuts and bolts of how a variation was worked on plot, how a twist on theme was threaded into the book. Perhaps it will spark an idea, some new slant you hadn't seen before. To analyze excellence starts you on the path toward excellence. Originality flows from putting your brain to work, forcing it to think in original terms. The work of master craftsmen can often provide the necessary stimulus.

At the same time, remember that nonfiction represents the raw material of a Western writer's novels. By immersing yourself in the history of the Old West, your imagination is exposed to a limitless source of plot material. Virtually every Western writer of my acquaintance spends part of his leisure time reading Western nonfiction. In my own case, hardly an evening passes that I don't read one or more chapters from a history book. The importance of reading nonfiction cannot be stressed too strongly. Let me illustrate with a story.

In 1971, I had yet to have a novel published. Three earlier efforts had collected a mass of rejection letters, and the situation looked bleak. Then, while reading one evening, I stumbled across a short passage in T. R. Fehrenbach's *Lone Star*. The reference was to Britt Johnson, a Texan whose family had been taken captive by the Comanches. The brief account noted that Johnson had made four trips into Comanche territory, which at the time was tantamount to suicide. Ultimately, he was able to ransom his own family as well as other captives. His daring and courage fired my imagination.

I began researching Britt Johnson. The more I learned, the more incredible the tale became. The concept for a novel took shape, and from that emerged a full-blown plot. The fictional account of Britt Johnson's heroism was published in 1972 under the title *Black Fox*. A relatively minor incident, buried in a history book on Texas, had resulted in my first published novel. In fact, every book I've written stemmed from something uncovered in Western nonfiction. Without exaggeration, there are thousands of such stories waiting to be told. Each in its own way has the dramatic punch of Britt Johnson's bold exploits. You have only to find the one that sparks your imagination.

The Suppose Game

Everything starts with a premise. From that initial idea there develops the nucleus of a story. Around that, situations are generated and characters gradually evolve. Bit by bit, piece by piece, it assumes dimension. There's a sense of events and people and drama. A plot.

Perhaps it won't come to you full-blown, as happened to me with Britt Johnson. On occasion you'll stumble across some nugget of information that presents no immediate story idea. Organize an idea file and begin collecting these odds and ends. Every now and then thumb through the file and refresh your memory. Allow yourself time to ruminate and play the Suppose Game. Suppose a particular incident was expanded in this way or that. Suppose several stray facts were put together to form a broader idea. Nothing monumental may occur to you at the moment. But the Suppose Game permits ideas to gestate. One day, when you least expect it, something sparks. You have the premise for a novel!

That's exactly how I got the premise for *The Kincaids*. For years I'd been collecting stray bits and pieces dealing with the settlement of Oklahoma. The idea for a novel was in there somewhere, but nothing concrete presented itself. Then, while crossing the Great Salt Lake Desert at night, it all came together. As I drove, I dictated a rough plot of the novel to my wife. She balanced a flashlight on the car seat and took it all down on a legal pad. Some two years later, in 1976, the novel was published in hardcover by Putnam. I couldn't count the number of times I'd played the Suppose Game and come up empty. Yet, in one night, *The Kincaids* emerged as a full-blown concept. Often as not, it happens just that way.

Some writers like to brainstorm their ideas with other writers. They verbalize the concept and then open it up for discussion. There's merit in this approach if you have profound respect for the other person's opinion. To solicit casual advice from family and friends might have an adverse effect. Their reaction to a partially developed concept might cause it to be stillborn. On several occasions I've sought the counsel of both my literary agent and my writing mentor. Still, I'm not in the habit of approaching them with all my ideas. For the most part, I ruminate and play the Suppose Game until a concept is crystallized. In the end, I believe a writer's vision is more important than anyone's opinion. That vision, the belief in oneself, is what creates novels.

Which leads again to the first step, structuring the novel. As you approach this critical stage, keep in mind that plotting is not finite. Instead, it's an ongoing process that requires both flexibility and versatility. The climax you originally envisioned may well prove unconvincing when you come to write it. Between the close of today's work and the start of tomorrow's you may revise the next scene in its entirety. A novel in progress undergoes constant change as characters and events take unforeseen turns. Stay alert and at all times be receptive to these sudden shifts. Some of your best plotting will be done in midstream.

Still another source of originality is your subconscious. Vivid images, sometimes disjointed images, spring from the depths of your mind. Even in a dreamlike state, when you're asleep, the mind flashes with images. The emotional force of these images often has intense dramatic impact. Be receptive, unleash your imagination no matter how crazy the image may appear at first glance. Let it germinate, work it around in your mind, play it out in a moment of fantasy. Perhaps it will never produce a unique concept, the idea for that great novel. Yet writers who achieve excellence have learned never to discard these oddball images. Originality is not necessarily the result of cognitive reasoning. Sometimes it emerges full-blown from nothing we can identify. Quickly here, quickly gone, unless you grab it on the instant.

Of course, when you start planning a book, the concept may not yet be wholly realized. The precise structure of the plot will be fuzzy and shapeless, too distant to grasp. Nonetheless, you have a point of departure. All you need is a means of getting from here to there, from beginning to end. So you're ready to consider a critical question.

How do you ride a horse?

Well, first, you catch the horse. Then you saddle it and mount and take control of the reins. A nudge of your heels gets the horse moving, and after that you adjust to the rhythm of the gait. Done right, you and the horse work in concert. No bouncing, no gall blisters, just a smooth ride.

What does all this have to do with writing a Western? The analogy is quite apt when we consider the matter of plotting. To construct a novel, you must first catch an idea. Then, in order to take control, you saddle it with vision and place yourself firmly astride the concept. Done right, a certain rhythm develops between you and the idea when things get moving. No lurching along, no mental traumas, just smooth writing all the way.

Nothing is quite that simple, of course. To ride a horse properly takes practice, and plotting a novel well comes only through experience. Essentially, a plot is a span of time in which people and events make things happen. The plot takes on life only when the writer introduces characters, thrusts them into the midst of events, and thereby sets the stage for action. To do all that, the writer needs a structure around which the whirligig will whirl. He needs a plot.

Structuring Your Story

There is no one way to plot a novel. Some writers believe that plotting an entire book would stifle their creativity. So they start with an idea, set the whirligig in motion, and let 'er rip. Characters enter at random, events occur in a storm of chaos, and the whole thing is chockful of digressions and irrelevancies. Theme seems nonexistent, the motives are weak, and the emotional impact of the story teeters in the balance. But the writer furiously writes on, for he considers the first draft nothing more than a circular outline. As the last page passes through the typewriter, he inserts Page One and commences pounding away on the second draft. He may write a third and a fourth draft, plugging holes in the plot and fleshing out characters each trip around. For many writers, it all comes together in the end.

In fact, quite a few of the Western writers I know work in just this manner. They may have a sketchy notion of who's involved and where it's headed and how it will get there. But their one imperative is the idea, the premise, the linchpin that connects characters and events. Some of them do miniplots, in effect winging it by structuring the book from scene to scene. Others simply uncork the bottle and let the demon of inspiration run where it will. The common denominator is that they all expect to do several drafts before the project is completed. From first draft to last, the manuscript may be cut from 500 pages to less than half that amount. No matter. Only the end result counts. And many superlative writers do it just that way.

The other way requires a somewhat more methodical approach. It's my way, not because I invented it, but only because it seemed the most logical way. When I began writing, I had no formal training in crafting novels. In fact, I had never met a novelist, much less spoken with one about the secrets of the trade. As a result, I was unaware that four or five drafts were considered essential to writing a good book. I thought the rational approach would be to lay it out in advance, construct a blueprint of sorts. To me, it seemed only reasonable that you get it right the first time.

Some three years later I discovered my error. Through my agent, I began meeting other writers, which led to discussions of things literary. I was astounded to learn that they pumped out three, four, even *five* drafts! Yet, at the same time, I met a few writers who considered "rewrite" a dirty word. Granted, they were in the minority, and thought to be somewhat strange. But curiously enough, their novels were as good as, in some cases better than, those written by the advocates of multiple drafts. I decided then that there's no one, sure-fire way of plotting a novel. There's only the way that's best for you.

In any event, here's how the "get it right the first time" school of thought works. To start, isolate the central idea for your novel and determine the theme. One supports the other, and together they form the backbone of the story. However, bear in mind that theme does not imply a "message." There is a tendency on the part of many writers to preach at their audience. They deliver long-winded lectures, through narrative and dialogue, on some moralistic crusade that has little to do with the story. Think of theme as the general subject of your novel, good versus evil being the classic example. Authors who climb up on soapboxes seldom get published.

The source of your story idea may have mixed origins. Perhaps you've invented a fictional character such as the Old West detective mentioned earlier. Or perhaps you're intrigued by an historical character, or an actual incident from the pages of history. Or you may want to tell the tale of a particular setting, such as ranch life or the fur trade. Whatever the source, your idea remains merely that until you've worked out a plot. You must structure a broad overview of what happens, a sequence of events.

A plot evolves in one of four ways: (1) The writer may borrow from some traditional plots, such as those used by Shakespeare. (2) He may choose to base the plot on the actual sequence of events involved in an historical incident. (3) With an initial situation in mind, he may construct the plot by working forward in time. (4) Starting at the end, with the climax the key element, he may work backward to the opening scene. Whichever method he selects, his priority does not change. He must now focus on the matter of climaxes.

Plot and Pace

The episodic pace of a Western is established through a series of climaxes which expand in intensity. As the story line advances, the writer must build into it periodic climaxes which excite and distress the reader. Along the way, he must determine the elements of drama and action needed to make each of those climaxes convincing. Lastly, the final climax should be not only credible but intriguing. The writer must figure out a way to make it at once inevitable and surprising. A climax that will startle the reader, make him blink.

Josh Logan, the playwright, once revealed his formula for good drama. He said: "In the first act, run your hero up a tree. In the second act, throw rocks at him. In the third act, get him down out of the tree." Though it's sound advice, it leaves the writer with the problem of first running his hero up a tree. Where do you start? How do you pinpoint the exact location of the tree? What happens to force the hero to grab for the lowest branch? All questions that have confounded and plagued storytellers of every persuasion. Yet the best solution is oftentimes the simplest solution.

The place to start is with a pencil and a pad of paper. Gather all your notes and research materials and scribbled reminders on the cast of characters. Segment everything by time frame, or chronological order, and jot it down on your pad. Simply putting it on paper provides some estimate of the span of time involved. Whether it's a week, a month, or ten years, you now have a basic framework. Of greater significance, you have an opening date—May 12, 1872—and by projection, a date the story ends. It's no longer illusory, or abstract. It's begun to look real, take shape and form.

Your next step is to separate the whole into a logical sequence of events. In life, everything revolves around cause and effect. One thing leads to another, what occurs today determines what happens tomorrow. You lay out a rudimentary plot in exactly the same manner. If you're working around an historical incident, then the events automatically assume a sequence. If your novel is wholly fictional, then it requires perhaps a bit more inventiveness. You must create events that provide sequential movement toward the ultimate climax. Give free rein to your imagination, but let it happen naturally. Life has more order than coincidence.

Your last step is to fill in the holes. Determine your major and secondary characters, and give them names. Decide who does what to whom and why. In other words, establish not only their actions but their motivations. Then figure out where and when those actions would most logically occur. Fit all that into the sequence of events until it dovetails with precision. Identify the climactic moments, and if necessary, rearrange them. What you're seeking is an episodic rhythm to the series of climaxes that will underscore conflict and heighten suspense. All else builds toward the final climax, and it must hurl the reader onward with ever greater velocity. When he gets there, actually reads those words, there must be *impact*. A collision of reader and event.

Don't confuse plotting with an outline of the plot. Some writers work out the entire plot in their head. Others use their notes and research materials to fashion a rough sequence of events. Still another group plots in detail, jotting down events, characters, and time frame. After the plotting stage, all of them must decide whether or not to construct a working outline. That subject will be covered at some length in Chapter 7, "The Mechanics of Storytelling." For now, suffice it to say that plotting is but one step toward an outline. Lots of ground must first be covered on the in-between stages.

The writer who plots in detail must also consider the matter of subplots. A subplot comprises a series of secondary events that nonetheless relate to the main story line. In traditional form, the subplot stems from the larger story and serves as background. Apart from enlivening the pace, and adding momentum, it serves to embellish the main plot. One essential purpose of the subplot is to provide broader revelations about the principal characters in the story. Jack Schaefer's use of the device in *Shane* stands as a masterful illustration. Shane's relationship with the sodbuster's wife never detracts from the impending showdown. Yet it does much to reveal the human side, the gentler aspects of a dangerous man.

For greatest effect, the characters of the subplot must be connected in some way to the main story. Usually one or more of the principal characters are involved in some fashion with the subplot characters. In this manner, added suspense can be created by stepping aside from the main plot for short intervals of time. Since constant tension is impossible to sustain, a subplot can also serve to lighten the mood here and there. Or, on the other hand, a subplot can be used to create a whole new set of hazards, and even greater suspense. As a standard practice, the subplot will be resolved before the novel's larger resolution. This tends to tighten the story line and provide a cleaner ending. Which brings our discussion full circle.

You now have the blueprint of a structure. Keep in mind that any blueprint can be changed any time the builder so desires. You are not bound to a rigid set of specifications. Nor does a plot constrict your imagination and stifle innovation. You can revamp it before you start writing, even in the midst of writing, and still again when you've finished writing. Let us return for a moment to the question of "How do you ride a horse?" Perhaps the most important step was that you take control of the reins. Pardon the mixed metaphors—blueprints and horses—but it all amounts to the same thing. You're the one in charge, the ramrod. The plot serves your will, not the other way round. It is, after all, a horse of your own creation.

To recap, all fiction is derivative. There are a limited number of plots, and each of them has been used thousands of times in past novels. A good writer turns this to advantage by adding twists to old conventions, presenting the familiar in unexpected ways. He must unveil the material from a new perspective, highlighting details other writers have failed to emphasize. Further, he must create a reality different from the conventional plot by continually surprising the reader. Imagination, innovation, the rat-a-tat-tat of your own drum.

In brief, the reader will anticipate what happens next based on novels he's read in the past. You, the writer, must factor that anticipation into the plotting and then avoid it. Fulfill those expectations instead in ways the reader *does not* anticipate. Plot to shock. To astound. To surprise. Give the reader what he wants, but startle him every now and then. And at the very end, make him blink.

Those last words are the most important words you will write. All that went before depends on the power of how you end it. Plot toward that final moment, the instant of impact. Jar the hell out of your reader.

Length and Symmetry

How do you plot the length of a Western? To a great extent, the length will be determined by the market category of the novel. Let's suppose you plan to write a traditional Western, the customary length being 70,000 words. Based on three hundred words per manuscript page, you can calculate the book at approximately 235 manuscript pages. Outlining the book, which I recommend, will enable you to structure the plot into chapters. By projecting the number of pages per chapter, you then know how many chapters the novel will contain. All of which raises another question. How many pages make a chapter?

I rarely write a chapter longer than 10 pages, and the scenes within a chapter vary from 4-6 pages. Some writers prefer shorter chapters, 6-7 pages, and thus a book of the same overall length will end up with more chapters. Other writers prefer longer chapters, broken down into four or five scenes, the length of each chapter running upwards of 20 pages. I experimented with all these techniques in early books and finally found the one that suits me best. As a general rule, you should write chapters of the length that you enjoy reading most.

There is no industry standard with regard to the length of chapters. However, in plotting the novel, you should keep several guidelines in mind. One of your principal goals is to create symmetry of structure, without rigidity or slow spots. The chapters should therefore be roughly equivalent in length. A 10-page chapter followed by a 7-page chapter followed by a 15-page chapter tends to disorient the reader. Vary the pace instead by varying the page length of scenes within a chapter. Whenever possible, use chapter breaks to shift the viewpoint from one character to another. That clean break usually works better than shifting viewpoint from scene to scene. Finally, chapter breaks are an excellent place to structure suspense into the plot. Ending a chapter with a cliffhanger or a character in emotional turmoil are but two examples. Uncertainty about what happens next prompts the reader to read on.

One last thought on chapter length. Traditional Westerns, as well as adult and series Westerns, are fast-paced and action-oriented. Thus the typical format calls for short chapters, usually 5-7 pages. Historical Westerns, or series Westerns presented as sagas, frequently have greater character development and a more involved story line. As a result, the chapter length on such books often exceeds 10 pages. Whether a chapter has viewpoint shifts, and two or more scenes, depends entirely on the author. Mainstream novels with a Western setting defy generalization. *Lonesome Dove,* which won a Pulitzer Prize, topped out at 843 pages. Some chapters ran 10 or more pages and others were 4-5 pages in length. Which only goes to prove that there are no hard and fast rules in writing. Excellence makes its own rules.

Tips on Plotting

What follows are some random thoughts about plotting Westerns. Any novel, whatever the genre, succeeds because the plot provides a framework for telling the story. A Western novel is at once the same and different. All the rules of good plotting must be followed. Yet a Western has certain dictates that do not apply to other genres. Here are a few observations, both general and specific, with regard to structuring the plot for a Western. Consider them carefully before you tackle your own novel.

■ Westerns suffer from the stereotype of mindless action and unmotivated violence. The term *shoot-'em-up* evolved from the old pulp school formula of at least one violent act every twenty pages. The absence of plot was compounded by the absence of a unifying theme. Yet a good novel, whether horse opera or historical saga, must have an underlying theme. For a theme is the thread that binds the story together. Nothing profound is required. Some of our classic Westerns have employed the universal theme of "good versus evil." Typical Western themes would include: Justice will out, The passing of the frontier, and Taming a raw wilderness. A writer must look upon theme as an integral part of plotting. To overlook it weakens the structure of any novel.

■ When crafting an historical novel, it is not enough to tell the reader what happened. A serious historical novelist will also examine *why* it happened, explore the deeper ramifications. In *The Kincaids*, I depicted how tribal lands were effectively stolen from the Five Civilized Tribes. The methods used by the government represented a story in itself. But the more important story was why these tribal lands were coveted by politicians and power brokers. Without the *why,* the reader would never have understood the reasons behind the settlement of Oklahoma. Historical novels obligate the writer to tell a complete story. The whole truth.

■ Chronology determines much of the story line in an historical Western. Dramatic and controversial events provide a literary springboard for the novel. The starting point can be selected within the chronology by working backward from the climactic event. Historical figures lend authenticity and need not necessarily play secondary roles. Fictional characters, of course, have the freedom to move about at will within the story. Their imagined adventures can be woven around the chronology of historical incidents. But the writer has an obligation to portray actual events and historical figures as accurately as possible. To put them where they weren't constitutes a historical juggling of time and place. To allow them to influence events in a fictional manner constitutes a reworking of history. Structure your plot to tell it the way it happened.

■ Early chapters in a novel must lay the foundation for what follows. Get your principal characters onstage, establish the situation, and provide the basis for conflict. By all means run your hero up a tree in the first third of the book (or sooner) and create some suspense. But your primary goal is to arouse the reader's interest, get him involved. When plotting your novel, organize the story line so that the opening chapter grabs the reader's attention. Intrigue him from the very outset with an unusual scene played out by compelling characters. Then proceed by gradual stages to lay the foundation for the balance of the novel. Too often, these elements are left unresolved until the actual writing. Your job will be simplified by working them into the story line during the plotting. Don't wait for inspiration to strike somewhere down the line. Do it now.

■ The element of quest plays a central role in all Western fiction. The quest of the mountain men into the fastness of the Rockies. The quest of the pioneers who crossed half a continent in wagon trains. The quest of the cattlemen to wrest the land from warlike tribes and establish ranching empires. The quest of the gunfighter, or shootist, for both respect and a measure of respectability. Clearly, the element of quest is one of the enduring attractions of the Western. To one degree or another, we all quest for meaning in our lives. Some achieve it by direct action. Others, perhaps the majority, achieve it vicariously. And the readers of Westerns are no exception. Allow them to live out their dreams through the exploits of your protagonist. Spice the plot with a liberal measure of quest.

■ A strong love story adds dimension to any novel. To start, it rounds out the central characters, makes them whole. Their inner feelings and vulnerabilities are part of what makes them human, and therefore more credible. Contrary to what you may think, male readers are vitally interested in the love life of the protagonist. Nothing syrupy or maudlin, but a solid love story with genuine emotion. Further, an element of romance provides the opportunity for working variations of conflict and suspense into the story line. As for sex, most readers prefer anticipation to the act itself. The intensity of the characters' needs and desires are more important than a graphic account. Finally, bear in mind that every Western novel considered to be a classic contained a love story involving the central characters. Strengthen your novel by adding romance to the plot. Emotion spices any good fiction.

■ Upheaval and disruption are basic elements of plotting. Upheaval of a seemingly stable situation works to surprise the reader and provoke greater interest. Suddenly turning things topsy-turvy also presents the opening for action, conflict, and suspense. Disruption of the characters' lives has great merit as a device to energize drama. Trouble and turmoil introduce an element of uncertainty, excite the reader. Unexpected disruption, occurring where the reader least anticipates it, heightens the overall impact of the story. These factors, upheaval and disruption, work best within the natural flow of events. Nothing contrived but rather an unforeseen turnabout that plays off some aspect of the story line. Plot to rattle the reader with orchestrated chaos.

You have several options with regard to plotting. Perhaps you will forego it altogether and simply uncork the demon of inspiration. That means you'll probably write three or four drafts of a novel before it's completed. Or maybe you'll opt for the methodical approach, structuring the book from beginning to end. Since that's my approach, I recommend it highly. Still, when it comes to the actual doing, you'll have to decide for yourself. Any book on writing can only review the ways it might be done.

However you decide, you will ultimately set the whirligig in motion. When you do, you'll meet some damned interesting people. And not a stranger in the bunch.

They're the characters in your novel.

NORTHERN PACIFIC R.R.
BUTTES
LONG LAKE CR.
BEAVER CR.
BOURBEUSE R.
FORT RICE
BATTLE CR.
RAMPART CR.
Elm R.
Maple R.
Village
MOREAU R.
Fox Island
LIT. SHEYENNE
BALBERO CR.
Pascals I.
Plum I.
Devils I.
Washte R.
New Fort Sully
SNAKE R.
MEDICINE KNOLL R.
Frozen Man
Old Ft Pierre
MISSOURI RIVER
SIOUX RES.
TORTOISE R.
DACOTA R.
Elm Cr
Ft SULLY
Cedar Cr.
Old Ft. George
MEDICINE HILL
INDIAN VILLAGE
Chanka
Winnebago Reserve
Medicine Cr.
American Crow
Red Cedar Cr.
YANKTON RESERVATION
Bad Land
South Fork
Oak Cr.
Two Tail
Dog Ears
Water Hole
Wetstone
Scalp Cr.
KEYA PAYA R.

3.
A Cast of Characters

Your task as a writer is to convince the reader that the events you've depicted actually happened. You provide such precision of detail about time and place that the reader believes the story to be true. In effect, the authenticity of the image persuades the reader to accept it as realism.

Yet accurate descriptions of events and places are merely the building blocks. How your characters behave, their emotions and their motives, are what moves the story from one scene to the next. Your primary function is to construct plausible characters, vividly sketched, who reveal themselves to the reader. Human emotions, not landscapes and cattle stampedes, convince the reader that you've written the truth.

You succeed when the reader ceases to be a passive observer. By layering detail upon detail, you induce the reader to become an active participant in the story. The agony and the ecstasy of your characters evokes a vicarious, very personal response from the reader. The printed page becomes, momentarily, an experience of enormous impact. Wholly engaged, the reader joins with the characters for an instant in time.

A good Western is a world come alive. The portrayal of characters, their dialogue and interaction, are etched with immediacy. Your vision transcends the word and becomes an image of clarity and motion within the reader's mind. Done well, the illusion assumes the shape of reality. All, for that instant in time, is truth.

To summon those images, you must write characters rather than caricatures. In the pulps, and the early days of paperback Westerns, the plot was the thing. The characters were little more than cardboard dummies used to keep the action humming along. What distinguished one from the other was the label pinned on them by the author. The reader was *told* who they were, rather than being shown. The result was a zany blend of caricature and stereotype.

Today, plot remains a primary concern of the novelist. What has changed over recent years is that characterization has assumed a position of equal billing. The modern reader of Westerns demands fully realized characters, flesh and blood rather than cardboard. That is not to say that a writer can shortchange plot in order to spotlight character. Think of them instead as co-stars. At all times, they share stage center.

Your goal as a writer is to strike a balance. Plot will determine what happens and when it happens and who does it. Characters will determine how it's done and why, and what effect it has on their lives. Yet the characters, like the plot, must be anchored in realism. However good the story, it will falter unless the characters are plausible, their actions believable. All of it must work in harmony, plot supporting characters and vice versa. One spotlight, stage center, illuminating both at once.

How does the writer strike a balance? The place to start is with your primary characters, the lead actors. You first have to know who they are, what makes them tick. Getting inside their heads requires that you develop a biography that includes age, background, physical description, mannerisms, and speech pattern. Further, the biographies must interlock, indicating the relationship of the characters to one another. A useful device for this task is a simple 3 × 5 card. Jot down the distinctive traits of each character on a separate card and spread them out on your desk. They'll soon begin to assume aspects of personality, the look of individuals.

Characters are often constructed from snippets of real people. In the course of your normal activities, you frequently run across someone who triggers a reaction. Stop and consider, ask yourself why you experienced that particular reaction. Identify the emotional trigger, perhaps a tone of voice or a physical trait. Commit it to paper and file it away under C for Characters. These everyday encounters will prove an invaluable aid when you come to people your novel.

The Star

The plot will determine what role your protagonist plays. Whether he's a cowhand or a gunfighter, you must now imbue him with human qualities. His height and weight, the color of his eyes and hair, are merely a starting point. To be credible, he must be whole and rounded, fleshed out. Perhaps he's resourceful and courageous, tough as whang leather. None of that stops him from being idealistic or sensitive, or even a bit flawed. A gunfighter who has nightmares takes on dimension, defies the stereotype. The point here is that real people are complex, creatures of paradox. Those contradictions, the imperfections, are what makes a character ring true. Nobody walks on water.

Yet your protagonist must be *admirable*. For all his imperfections, he can never lose the sympathy of the reader. He must prove worthy of his adversaries, those who will try his mettle. At the same time, he must be smart as well as brave, employing his brain as often as he does his fists or a gun. The overriding theme of the Western genre is that justice will prevail. So, in the end, the reader must believe that your protagonist is admirable, somehow valiant. A man equal to the task.

Get your protagonist onstage early in the story. Work out an opening scene that will immediately establish him as a man of action. Not that it has to be a slugfest or a shootout, or anything heroically dynamic. But it does have to make him memorable from the beginning, someone who stands out in a crowd. Let something happen that will give the reader a picture to remember. A visual image that will stick in the mind throughout the book. Here's how I introduced Clint Brannock in *Windward West*. The scene takes place in a saloon filled with buffalo hunters and soldiers.

> *Other men seldom intruded on Clint. He was tall and solidly built, with wind-seamed features and a wide brow. His manner was deliberate, which combined with a square jaw and smoky blue eyes gave him a standoffish appearance. He generally drank alone, and while he was pleasant enough, most men kept their distance. He allowed them the same courtesy.*

Not an elaborate description, but it performs a serviceable job. The reader now has a mental image of Clint, and reason to believe he could be a dangerous man. The fact that other men keep their distance indicates he has earned their respect, if not their friendship. Further, there's a hint of complexity to his character, something not yet revealed. All these things are like brush strokes in the mind of the reader. A first impression that will assume dimension as the story progresses.

An indirect method of character revelation often has even more impact on the reader. In effect, we see aspects of one character through the eyes of another. A. B. Guthrie employed the technique with great skill throughout *The Big Sky*. Here, we are observers as Jim Deakins, a mountain man, reflects on his partner and the protagonist of the novel, Boone Caudill.

> *For all that he gave in to Boone, Jim felt older and a heap wiser and he knew that Boone depended on him. Some ways, Boone was like a boy still, needing just a careful word to be dropped to see things right and wise. Shooting buffalo or catching beaver or fighting bear, Boone was as good as the best, but with people it was different. He didn't know how to joke and give and take and see things from different sides and to find fun instead of trouble. All he knew was to drive ahead.*

As readers, we now have greater insight into Boone Caudill. We know that his abrasive manner, and his troubles with other mountain men, stem from an inability to shrug off any real or imagined slight. He reacts heedlessly rather than thinking a situation through. Yet, with someone he respects, he's open to counsel, willing to accept advice. The passage works because it's character revelation with subtle brush strokes. The reader has no awareness that images have been summoned by the writer. Yet he understands the protagonist infinitely better than he did a moment before. Boone Caudill has assumed dimension.

Of course, some readers prefer a heroine to a hero. Traditionally, the protagonist of a Western has been male. However, there are any number of fine novels, set in the West, with a female lead. All the rules of good characterization apply, with no token allowances for the "weaker sex." The ladies of the Old West were just as rugged as their male counterparts. And oftentimes a damnsight tougher! I refer you to the novels of Lucia St. Clair Robson and Jeanne Williams. Their female protagonists are worth the reading.

The Co-Star

The antagonist, or villain, must be portrayed in much the same manner. No man is wholly evil, sinister through and through. Perhaps he's callous and brutal, a coldblooded killer, thoroughly reprehensible. But carried to the extreme it becomes melodramatic, just another caricature. The antagonist, to be plausible, must possess the foibles and flaws of humankind. Some aspect of his character must make him vaguely sympathetic, if not likeable. In short, a badman we love to hate.

A well-drawn antagonist will be conniving and clever, though not necessarily a tower of intelligence. While he knows right from wrong, his values are skewed, somehow at odds with conventional beliefs. He thinks in terms of self-interest, winning at any cost, and therefore exhibits a certain arrogance toward the world in general. From his warped perspective, he believes himself immune to the laws that govern normal men. He considers himself superior, so crafty as to be invincible. He likes what he sees in the mirror.

But all that represents only one side of the man. To be a fully realized character, he must also possess some ordinary qualities. Too often the villain in a Western displays no emotion, none of the sentiment or passion of everyday life. He has no family ties, no wife or lady friend, no one to share his repugnant dreams. He consorts instead with whores and assorted dregs of humanity. This total absence of any redeeming quality makes him less credible, not whole. He is a cardboard cutout painted black. A classic stereotype.

Which is not to say that the antagonist should be plumbed in great depth. But rather that he should be portrayed as a whole man, with some regard to motivations and inner thoughts. Let action and dialogue depict his ruthlessness, his contempt for the law and the law-abiding. Underneath that dispassionate exterior, show some grain of normal feelings, some vestige of a heart. Give him dimension simply by sketching traits other than brutish cruelty. In *Bloodstorm*, I brought the villain onstage during a routine business meeting. A lawyer in the book, he was based on an actual historical figure who ruled New Mexico Territory.

> *The man behind the desk was short and thickset. Somewhere in his late forties, he had the girth of one who indulged himself in all the good life had to offer. He was clean shaven, with round features and thin hair combed back over his head. His eyes were deep-set and shrewd, and his smile was patently bogus. He rose as they entered the office.*

There's little to suggest that Stephen Elkton is the ringleader of a conspiracy, a man who orders other men killed. Ostensibly an upstanding citizen, he seems upon first meeting a powerful but somewhat benign figure. His sinister methods are later revealed through dialogue and the murderous acts he engineers. The extent of his ruthlessness becomes apparent to the reader only gradually, layer by layer. Like many truly evil men, his outward appearance hardly fits the part. He seems instead quite ordinary.

Supporting Cast

Other primary characters are crafted with the same attention to detail. The list might include anyone who plays a major role in the story. There are two determining factors: their importance to the plot and the extent of their relationship with the protagonist. They must be brought to life with a fine touch, vividly sketched. In point of fact, they are no less essential to the book than the protagonist and the villain. How they behave, the degree to which they are credible characters, becomes a vital element in the success of any novel. They must be full-blown and life-like, very real to the reader.

Elmer Kelton's *The Good Old Boys* takes place in the West Texas country of 1906. The protagonist, Hewey Calloway, drifts into his brother's ranch after a long absence. The reunion leads to a scene with his sister-in-law, who becomes a principal character in the story. Kelton masterfully creates an impression that will linger in the reader's mind.

> *Eve Calloway was well into her thirties, no longer really young but not yet reconciled to pass over that one-way threshold into middle age. She was at a time in her life when with the right clothes and activated by the right mood she could still seem girl-like, years younger than her actual age. Or, if tired and irritable and taking no care for her appearance, she could look years older than she was. Hewey had seen her both ways so many times he never knew which to expect.*

Depicted here is a woman any Westerner would recognize. Her years on the West Texas plains have taken their toll. No actual physical description is rendered in this particular passage. Yet we sense that the hard life on a ranch, constant exposure to the elements, has left her worn. At the same time, there is the suggestion of a spirited woman, older but still attractive. The reader now has a distinct image of Eve Calloway.

The Bit Players

Secondary characters pose an interesting problem for the writer. These are characters who revolve around the protagonist and the villain, as well as the other primary characters. They are bit players whose principal function is to people the world you've created in the novel. Their roles can be acted out either within the main plot or within the various subplots. They are memorable more for what they do than for who they are.

Avoid a cast of thousands when creating secondary characters. Too many people running here and there simply complicate the story and confuse the reader. Moreover, space limitations severely restrict the on-stage time of these bit players. You must profile them with sharp, swift lines, economical brush strokes. Keep in mind, you're writing a Western, not a character study. Get them onstage and off in an expeditious manner.

To write a secondary character, focus on some singular aspect that captures the individual. A device that works rather well is to let the role define the character. Not all undertakers are cadaverous and not all bankers are portly gentlemen with jowls. But the role will often suggest physical appearance, type of dress, and personal traits. Then, to round out the character, show him on the job, in the bank or the funeral parlor. Set him in motion and let him perform according to the dictates of the scene. Structure the dialogue so that he reveals something of himself when he talks.

Since time is at a premium, you must make a lasting impression when a secondary character first appears onstage. Later, when he makes another appearance, there's seldom an opportunity to jiggle the reader's memory. So the portrait must be sharply etched at the moment of introduction. Elmer Kelton performed the task with crisp economy in *The Good Old Boys*. He even managed to add a touch of humor.

> *His name was Frank Gervin. Behind his back, people referred to him by a boyhood nickname, "Fat," but the tactful and prudent never called him that to his round and ruddy face.*
> *Hewey said, "Howdy, Fat."*

In a few lines, the character has been distinguished with swift and certain strokes. The reader is unlikely to forget Frank "Fat" Gervin, and there's reason to believe that most people hesitate to incur his wrath. The reader also learns something more about Hewey Calloway. He's neither tactful nor prudent. Instead, he's a bit of a prankster.

Walk-On Roles

One last category of characters deserves mention. These are the minor characters, actors who perform walk-on roles throughout the story. They pop into the book without fanfare and pop out just as quickly. Their function is to provide background and color rather than to advance the plot. Yet, like any character, they must be drawn convincingly.

The description of a minor character is necessarily brief. A short paragraph, sometimes a single sentence, will suffice. The bartenders and storekeepers of Westerns are not meant to dazzle or amaze. Their purpose is to be in the right place at the right time, and to say whatever needs saying to keep things moving. For all that, minor characters should never be slighted. A scene in Dee Brown's *Conspiracy of Knaves* provides an excellent illustration.

> *As twilight was darkening the busy street outside a window of the barroom, the messenger arrived. He was a furtive little man, slightly hunchbacked, exposing broken yellow teeth in a grimace when he handed Major Heywood a brown envelope and turned away toward the exit in a motion that reminded Colonel Eberhart of a scuttling cockroach.*

The messenger was onstage only a moment. The overall scene would have worked with no physical description of such a minor character. Yet it worked infinitely better because the messenger assumed shape and form, some aspect of singularity. Details are the marrow of good writing, and even a walk-on role must be handled with skill. Here, with considerable craft, one sentence sufficed to create a graphic impression.

Directing the Show

Some writers dominate their characters with an iron hand. They believe it's essential to govern every action, every word of dialogue, in order to keep the story line on track. These are writers who generally plot the novel in advance and construct a detailed outline. However, there are writers who do little in the way of plotting and still take a disciplinarian attitude toward their characters. Either group has deep concern that unmanageable characters would take the book off course and thereby depart from the writer's original intent. They adhere to a rigid concept that allows no deviation.

Writers of this persuasion usually share a common trait. Before starting the book, they perform an in-depth analysis of each character. What they do should not be confused with a character sketch or a personality profile or a biography. Their analysis plumbs the psyche of each character: emotion and motivation, habits and idiosyncrasies, interrelationships with every other character. They know these people better than they know themselves before committing a word to paper. No one can say with any authority that their approach is either right or wrong. What works for them works very well indeed. Fine novels are crafted in just this manner.

A great many writers take the opposite approach. Their attitude toward characters is somewhat more personal, even intimate. They believe every character has a mind and a soul, a spiritual form merely waiting to be born on paper. Further, they believe that characters are individualists, possessing a will of their own. The writer therefore adopts a benevolent outlook, allowing the characters great latitude and freedom of action. The writer maintains a degree of control, for complete anarchy would lead to chaos. But he listens carefully to what his characters say. He lets them tell him what happens next.

I subscribe to this school of thought. Though I construct a detailed outline, I believe some mystical bond exists between writer and character. To me, these are flesh-and-blood people, corporeal and real, with distinct voices. As I begin the day's stint at the typewriter, they gather around me, not just visualized but visible. We converse, sometimes we argue, and they are frank to express an opinion as to how a scene should be played out. I respect their views, and grant them enormous leeway, for it is their lives being depicted. All this may sound a tad farfetched, even whimsical. I can only say it's real to me, and it never ends. The characters from my books are with me even now, here today. They nod in agreement as I write these lines.

Several writers of my acquaintance think I'm a bit skewed. Yet I know just as many others who share a similar bond with their characters.

They believe, as I do, that removing the leash from characters adds both spontaneity and realism to the story. Characters assume a life of their own, dictate their own behavior, and write their own dialogue. Of course, with such independent characters, the writer has to remain flexible. Scenes veer off on a tangent never intended by the writer. The plot, midway through the book, often requires major revision. But all that's to the good, and ultimately improves the story. These willful, unruly characters are actually living the moment. They know what they would or would not do in a given situation. The writer's role is to listen closely and record it accurately. He scribes a story told by the characters themselves.

Let me illustrate the point. *The Savage Land* was my third published novel. Print Oliver, the protagonist, returns from the Civil War to find that his mother now rules the family ranch. In the outline, I fully indended that the mother would relinquish control only after a bitter struggle. I visualized high drama in an adversarial relationship between Julia Oliver and her eldest son. When it came time to write their first clash, Julia Oliver suddenly bowed her neck and refused to follow orders. She told me, in no uncertain terms, that she was not a tough-as-nails tyrant who coveted power. I acceded to her demands and recorded the loving manner in which she established Print as head of the family. Julia proved to be a woman of wisdom and understanding, a source of inspiration for her children. With me, however, she exerted her will and insisted that her character be portrayed accordingly. The book was enhanced by her determination to be herself.

Keep in mind, I'm not advocating my way as the only way. I suspect most writers take a middle-ground approach. They give their characters a fairly loose leash but they still retain control. Scenes occasionally veer off course and the plot sometimes takes an unexpected twist. For the most part, however, these middle-ground writers know where they're headed and everything that will happen along the way. Their characters are like headstrong children who must be encouraged, oftentimes manipulated, to toe the mark and perform on cue. Perhaps, in the end, such writers have the best of both worlds. They are neither rigid disciplinarians nor practitioners of freewheeling improvisation. Their work progresses along predictable lines, with only minor detours. No jarring surprises for them.

Certain writers I know take a vicarious approach to characterization.

Somewhat like an actor playing a role, they step into a character's part whenever he appears onstage. They imagine themselves to be that character at that particular moment in time. Every word of dialogue, the character's actions and reactions, are acted out by the writer. By getting inside the character, the writer delivers a performance that comes from within. The tricky part occurs when a writer moves from character to character within the same scene. An aspect of multiple personality too dizzying to contemplate must leave the writer thoroughly drained at the end of the day. For all that, the method works exceptionally well for some writers. They are, in effect, their characters.

Other writers purposely adopt an impersonal attitude. They put a psychic distance between themselves and their characters. For them, the story takes precedence; they believe intimate acquaintance with characters might sidetrack them from that larger goal. While it's strictly one man's opinion, I've always found that attitude to be counterproductive. A writer who never gets one-on-one with his characters generally writes lifeless mannequins who plod through their roles. Perhaps he tells a whale of a story, packed with action and hairpin twists to the plot. But he leaves the reader wondering who those people were and why the hell they ever got themselves involved. There's a comic strip quality to it, nothing memorable or satisfying. Quickly read and quickly forgotten.

Still, there's no right or wrong way. An audience exists for every form of Western, from slam-bang horse operas to literate explorations of our frontier past. Every writer must decide how much of himself he's willing to invest in his characters. That decision will in turn determine what approach he takes to characterization. Personally, I've always harbored a certain envy of the disciplinarians, middle-grounders, and comic strip writers. At night, when they shove back from the typewriter, they leave their characters imprisoned in paper. Mine follow me wherever I go, grumbling until I once more get on with telling their story. I like 'em, but Judas Priest—sometimes they're real pests!

On Skirts and Spurs

Writers by necessity are students of human nature. Nowhere does that study serve so well as when we're writing about the opposite sex. A male writer, writing about women, must tell the story from a woman's point of view. The trick is to see it through her eyes, experience it through the

45

prism of her emotions. And it works vice versa as well. A woman writer, dealing with a male character, must step into his boots, spurs and all. Sounds simple enough, doesn't it?

Any experienced writer will tell you it's a formidable proposition. *Mattie Silks*, my second published novel, was a fiction-based-on-fact account of the Old West's most famous madam. Her association with Wild Bill Hickok and other notorious figures promised to be a compelling tale. I wrote the book without pause or reservation, confident I had captured the essence of this remarkable woman. When my wife read the manuscript, she was at first noncommittal. Later, after I insisted on honesty, she informed me that the male characters were very credible, real people. But the protagonist of the story, Mattie Silks, was a one-dimensional stick figure. No woman reader, my wife advised, would identify with the pivotal character of the book. Mattie Silks simply hadn't been brought to life!

All that candor forced me to do some serious thinking. *Mattie Silks* was already sold, and the publisher expressed no need for revisions. But I was convinced that my wife's arguments were sound. To revamp my outlook, I began reading the diaries and journals of frontier women, as well as novels written by women for women. Further, when I came to write about other female characters, I shifted mental gears and consciously tried to look at the world from their perspective. Then, as a sort of litmus test, I asked my wife and various women friends to critique what I'd written. This do-it-yourself program paid off somewhere around the fifth book. Apart from my wife, lady editors and women readers now agree that I write plausible female characters. Not as good as the male characters, but fully realized nonetheless. I take that as high praise.

The point requires no great elaboration. Good writing dictates that every character in your book have a flesh-and-blood immediacy. Unless you were born with remarkable sensitivity, that means you have to be more than a casual student of human nature. Women writers, as well as men writers, must actively educate themselves in the values and cultural differences of their opposites. If nothing else, pride of craft should start you on a program of enlightenment. Failing that, allow a member of the opposite sex to critique your female (or male) characters.

Gawdalmightydamn! You'll soon get the message.

Imaginary vs. Real Life

Some characters are drawn from our everyday experiences. Observation enables a writer to create characters whose looks and behavior are patterned on actual people. Yet no character is the literal embodiment of a real-life prototype. The most skilled "people watcher" will never capture the whole person on paper. As writers, we interpret what we've seen and filter it through our imaginations. We then reinvent the actual person to fit the needs of our fictional character. The underlying factor has to do with the writer's mental image of a particular character. Only by the greatest coincidence would a real-life person serve as the exact counterpart of that image. To prove the point, try using one of your relatives as a character in a novel. You'll quickly discover an imperfect match. Writers merely observe people. We *create* characters.

At times, of course, our creations emerge from the subconscious mind. Characters are quite often composites of various people we've known in everyday life. We combine the appearance of one with the speech pattern of another and add the oddities of behavior of yet a third. A part of this mixing and molding might be done on a conscious level. But the larger part flows from a source we rarely recognize. All of which reinforces the value of "people watching." Our subconscious mind is a repository of information and impressions. Every aspect of writing depends to some extent on experiences we've warehoused throughout our lives. Characterization profits immeasurably when we listen closely to that inner voice. For in the end, emotion powers fiction. And characters are the wellspring of all emotion.

Plot sets the stage. A writer's skill at characterization personalizes the story, engages the reader. When characters are fully drawn the reader comes to care about them. He identifies with them, experiences an emotional tug of concern for their welfare. A part of that concern has to do with how they resolve their conflicts. The greater part has to do with how their lives turn out. An engaged reader always hopes for the best.

Editors are no less susceptible. In early 1976, I turned in the manuscript for *The Kincaids*. A week or so later I got a frantic phone call from the editor at Putnam. Her first words were: "My God! You've killed Jake!" She was two-thirds of the way through the manuscript and had just read the passage where Jake Kincaid, the family patriarch, had been killed. Her reaction was one of emotional distress, for at that point she genuinely cared about Jake. For my part, I was pleased as hell. I had my editor hooked!

Tips On Characterization

No one book can tell you everything about characterization. Here are some personal observations, the product of living with characters who assumed their own identities. For want of a better definition, let's call it one writer's tips of the trade. These are thoughts to bear in mind as you people your novel and during the actual writing itself. Thoughts that will help bring your characters alive.

■ To create a cast of characters, start with one person. A pivotal character generates other primary characters who in turn generate secondary characters. Or start with an idea, the germ of a story. Ideas spawn situations, and situations strung together form a story line. Characters will then emerge, stepping onstage as the plot thickens. Before you know it, you'll have a complete cast.

■ Introduce your principal characters early on in the book. There is no hard and fast rule as to how soon the protagonist should be introduced. However, in general, the quicker your lead character gets onstage, the quicker the reader will become wholly involved in the story. Secondary characters can be introduced at a more leisurely pace. Usually, it's best to bring them onstage at intervals, one at a time. Don't overwhelm the reader with a blur of faces and a latticework of relationships. Take the gradual approach to building your cast of characters. Impress them on the reader's memory by making their introduction somehow distinctive.

■ The biography you create for a character is designed principally as a source of reference. All the material about the character—family, background, and past experiences—does not have to be jammed into the book itself. For the most part, the biography is a means of getting to know the character before you actually start writing. Then, as the book progresses, it serves as a ready reference that enables you to keep the character in character. No thumbing back a hundred pages to verify that he's bald as a billiard ball and nearsighted. You have the information at your fingertips.

■ Think of yourself as casting director for a movie. You would never select actors, either male or female, who are look-alikes. What you want in a cast of characters is variety. Variety in physical appearance, speech patterns, and mannerisms. Characters should also differ from one another in terms of temperament. Otherwise they're nothing more than stick figures spouting dialogue in the same voice.

■ Strive for contrast in characters, the juxtaposition of opposites. A simple example would be two men who are steadfast friends: one is brash and assertive, but no mental giant; the other is quiet but strong, a persuasive leader. Contrast in personality presents the opportunity for differing attitudes and opinions. Moreover, it allows the reader to see the world you've created through differing points of view. All that combines to provide added texture to the story.

■ People your novel with characters who are *characters*. Nobody wants to read about the All-American Boy or The Girl Next Door. These are characters we've known all our lives. As readers, we want characters who are unordinary, somehow unique. Characters who engage or titillate or provoke. We are fascinated by eccentricity.

■ Erect barriers between your characters and what they covet most. Obstacles raise the spectre of trouble, and readers love trouble. An obstacle surmounted makes the goal worthwhile. A protagonist who surmounts the obstacle—overcomes trouble—takes on dimension and stature. How the character responds to adversity and challenge serves as a revelation, absorbs the reader.

■ Frustration can also be used to reveal character. An unexpected obstacle, some barrier or challenge, creates ongoing peaks of interest. The average reader is never more fascinated than when a beleaguered hero comes face to face with a stone wall. Human nature wants to see adversity turned to advantage, but not without a little frustration. A low point for the protagonist will rarely fail to spark intense involvement for the reader.

■ Don't expect your reader to wade through page after page of introspection. As a literary device, the inner monologue is designed as a means of character revelation. The primary purpose is to reveal aspects of the character's personality to the reader. The secondary purpose is to pass along plot information through the thoughts of the character. Save the philosophy and all that abstract, deep-think stuff for bull sessions with friends. Your reader isn't interested in your world view, past or present. He just wants you to get the hell on with the story.

■ A character who acts is far more compelling than one who thinks and thinks and thinks. Allow your character a moment of introspection, but have him do something *while* he's reflecting. Let him pace the floor, or knock back a shot of whiskey, or saddle a horse. Then, in the midst of the action, allow him to reflect and ponder the imponderable. But only briefly; take every shortcut possible to arrive at the point of his introspection. Taking the long-way-round will foment rebellion in your readers. They'll skip pages until your character does something, *anything*. Permit them to watch rather than forcing them to listen. They want action, not angst.

A final observation. How you coexist with your characters will determine how you approach characterization. Perhaps you'll hold them at arm's length, or rule them with an iron hand. Perhaps they'll assume shape and identity and take control of their own lives. However it works out, never forget that emotion powers fiction. You must somehow portray the emotion of your characters, capture it on paper. Only then will they step off the page with flesh-and-blood immediacy.

Of course, their emotion must be expressed. Anger and grief and joy cannot be revealed solely through inner monologue. To be fully realized, characters must express their feelings to someone besides themselves. They must articulate their thoughts.

Simply stated, they must talk. But more to the point, they must talk like Westerners. So let's talk about how they'll talk.

It's called dialogue.

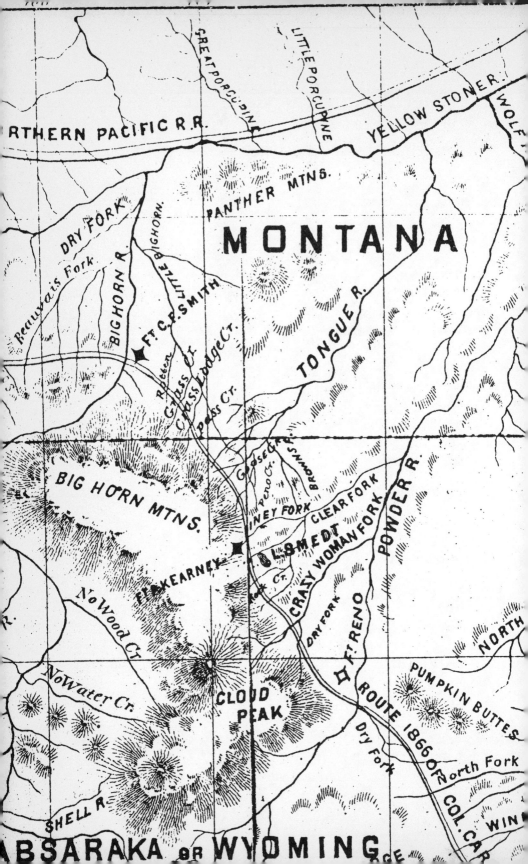

4. Writing Western Dialogue

The way characters talk sets the tone of a novel. Their spoken words, even more than the narrative, make the thrust of the story credible. No amount of description will convince the reader that the characters are real. They must speak before they can assume life, that all important flesh-and-blood immediacy. What they say and how they say it determines whether the reader believes what they do, their actions. Dialogue is the great persuader of fiction.

Westerns present still another challenge. There's a sort of cowboy lingo associated with the way Westerners talk. The reader expects Western characters to say such things as "howdy" and "much obliged" and "pronto." Yet the Old West was no less populated by immigrants and settlers, not to mention the widespread influence of Mexicans. Diverse cultures were represented throughout the West, and any true depiction will reflect their differences. Not everyone savvied cowboy lingo.

For all that, a writer of Westerns must begin somewhere. Cowboy lingo plays a role in the mythical West, and therefore establishes a traditional form of expression. One way to acquire a working knowledge of the vernacular is to read Westerns. When you come across dialogue that rings true, analyze the words and how they were used. All dialogue begins with words, and in this case, many of the words were unique to the time and place. By studying a good dialogist's style, you develop an awareness of how Westerners expressed themselves in everyday conversation. You'll shortly discover that it has a particular sound.

Here's an example from Elmer Kelton's *The Good Old Boys*. Hewey Calloway, the protagonist, shows up at his brother's place after a long absence. The moment is one of deep emotion, and they silently hug each other. At length, the brother speaks.

"The prodigal son," Walter exulted, "finally come home. And there's not a fatted calf on the place."

"I'd settle for a wing from a drouthy quail."

"You may have to." Walter stepped back for a good long look at Hewey, from his face to his thorn-scarred boots. "I'd about decided you'd finally found a bronc you couldn't ride or a cow you oughtn't to 've roped. Thought they'd buried you someplace without us knowin' it. You had three years of schoolin'. Didn't you learn to write?"

"Not to where you could read it."

Anyone from West Texas would recognize either of these men. Kelton has captured a cadence of speech common to people from that part of the country. The choice of words and how those words are framed also combine to create superior dialogue. The last line, spoken by Hewey Calloway, could have been phrased in many different ways. But his truncated, self-deprecating "Not to where you could read it" rings true to the people and the place. Hewey and Walter come alive by their own words. They talk the way they should talk.

Western lingo amounts to a specialized vocabulary. Your dialogue will further improve by studying three excellent reference sources. *Western Words* by Ramon Adams and *A Dictionary of the Old West* by Peter Watts present a knowledge of the idiom found nowhere else. The third source, *Dictionary of American Slang,* provides definitions of words as well as historical usage. For the Western writer, these volumes represent a window into the past. Apart from serving as a ready reference, they also allow you to educate yourself in a vocabulary that was unique to the era. Add them to your library before you begin writing Western dialogue.

Spoken Revelations

Of course, words are merely the starting point. You proceed from there by recognizing that dialogue serves many functions. Interspersed with narrative, it advances the story. Characters discuss what's happened, or speculate on future plans, and thereby set the stage for what happens next. Their dialogue advances the story by leading the reader into an action sequence, another passage of narrative, or the following scene. As the characters converse, it also provides a forum for an interplay of ideas. Whereas narrative can present ideas, dialogue enables characters to analyze, express opinions, and provide insights into people and situations. Further, through their own words, characters assume personality and dimension. They take shape as individuals by expressing their thoughts. In a sense, dialogue is an intricate sort of needlework. It stitches together loose pieces of narrative and binds them into a whole. When it's done well, the stitches never show.

A scene from Dee Brown's *Conspiracy of Knaves* illustrates the point. In total, the scene is almost eight pages long, with roughly three pages of narrative and five pages of dialogue. Two of the primary characters, after a tense meeting with several other characters, make their exit from a hotel room. The final passage, which is virtually all dialogue, leads the reader directly into the next scene. Here's the way it ends.

> *Marianna suppressed a gasping outcry that brought Truscott quickly to her side. Taking her arm, he led her through the door and into the hall.*
>
> *"Come along," he said. "I believe I know where we may find Charley."*

Dee Brown advances the story by ending the scene with cleverly constructed dialogue. Yet the cleverness, like those hidden stitches mentioned earlier, doesn't show. The scene ends at a natural point—the exit from the hotel room—and sets the stage for the following scene. The reader keeps reading because he's interested to see what happens when Marianna and Truscott find Charley. The transition between scenes was accomplished by the simple device of double-spacing and then proceeding with the story. All in all, it's a workmanlike job of using dialogue to move things along.

Dialogue serves varied functions for a central reason. Apart from expanding the story, dialogue interests and intrigues readers. There's a bit of the eavesdropper in all of us; we like to "overhear" people talking. Human nature prompts us to eavesdrop on people wherever we go, even in the most commonplace situations. While we're reluctant to admit it, we have an innate curiosity about the lives of total strangers. Similarly, we enjoy listening to the characters in a book. Their conversation makes us privy to their plans and problems. Their secrets.

In fact, dialogue reveals the nature of a character in a direct manner. The reader is being shown rather than told what makes a character tick. Properly structured, a passage of dialogue often provides greater insights than several pages of narrative. We learn how a character thinks and what he intends, his motives and motivations. Whether he's sneaky or sincere, weak or tough, will be revealed by what he says. His words mark him in our minds.

On another level, dialogue works as action. Simply by talking, the characters are doing something, making things happen. Their conversation draws the reader into the story and creates a sense of vicarious involvement. Dialogue personalizes events, whereas narrative frequently has about it an element of the impersonal. The reader comes to care about characters, or despise them, through who they are and how they behave. Nothing divulges more about them than the words out of their own mouths. Yet, at the same time, their talk actionizes the story. They're leading the reader onward even as they speak.

Too much dialogue, of course, serves to impede the story. The writer must strike a fine balance between dialogue and narrative, which includes action sequences. Overlong conversations between characters lose punch and risk losing the reader's interest. When it's merely talk, without advancing the story or providing revelation, then it ceases to function effectively. Good dialogue must be sharp rather than meandering, moving with some dispatch to the point of the conversation. As a general rule, it must show the reader something that bears directly on either character or story. Otherwise, it needs reworking with a red pencil.

Pitfalls of Dialect

Still another hazard has to do with phonetic spelling of words. The writer's purpose is to faithfully reproduce dialects or regional accents on paper. How it sounds to the ear and how it looks in print are often totally at odds. When it forces a reader to translate as he reads, then it loses the desired impact. The better way would be to achieve the effect by accenting selected words, just a sprinkling of dialect. A little bit does the trick, whereas too much quickly defeats the reader. Here's a short passage from A. B. Guthrie's *The Big Sky*, which illustrates the technique. The father, addressing his son, Boone Caudill, speaks a dialect that's still readable.

*"I told you onc't to hush, but no, by God, you got to have
your say! I ain't just tellin' you ag'in." Pap gave Boone a shove.
"If'n you leave, the law'll draw you back. Git outside!"*

Whenever possible, avoid the use of dialect. However, if you must use it,
then you're obligated to make it consistent throughout. Dialect must be
spelled phonetically to capture the inflections, and that requires constant scrutiny on the writer's part. Different versions of the same word
or expression will confuse the reader and produce unintended clashes of
sound. Moreover, too much dialect forces the reader to decipher dialogue, particularly when several characters speak in what seems a foreign tongue. The reading then becomes a tedious mental exercise rather
than entertainment. You're writing a novel, not a crossword puzzle.
Don't overdo dialect.

Bloody Hand was my fifth published novel. Fiction based on fact, it
was the story of mountain man Jim Beckwith. I was fascinated by Beckwith in particular and mountain men in general. Moreover, I felt com-
pelled to depict these rugged individualists as they actually were. That
led to a peculiar dialect which was unique to the Western experience.
Nowhere else was there a language such as that spoken by the mountain
men. Here's a passage of dialogue involving Beckwith and another character, Doc Newell.

*Newell's belly bounced with rumbling laughter. "Christ
A'mighty, I'm hyar to tell ye we had a year, Jimbo. Hump meat
in the pot nigh onto every day, and more blasted beaver'n ye
could beat off with a club. Yore lookin' at a rich man, young'n.
Made 'em come, I did!"*

*"Wal, braggin' ain't my specialty, ye'll recollect, but we
didn't exactly pull up empty-handed our own selves. Davey Jackson ain't no one to share a cave with, but that coon shore out-
shines the rest of his bunch. Brung in twenty-three packs, we did,
and nary a pelt among 'em won't go fer prime."*

The entire book, all 352 pages, contains similar dialogue. To put it as
charitably as possible, I got carried away with mountain man dialect.
The reader needed a translator every time one of the characters opened
his mouth. Since all the characters spoke this arcane language, the pace

of the novel was slowed by the ongoing mental translation. Given the chance to rewrite *Bloody Hand*, I would cut the dialect by half. Yet it serves as an excellent illustration of how not to structure dialogue around dialect. Don't let your enthusiasm for the unusual override your common sense. Treat dialect with wary respect.

Speech Patterns

Keep in mind as well that dialogue differs from everyday conversation. People tend to ramble on and string together incomplete sentences in real life. Characters in novels have to say it crisply and with clarity, every word serving a purpose. Moreover, when it's written out, the reader doesn't *hear* the inflection in a character's voice. Italics can be used sparingly to stress words, but overuse usually works to distract the reader. Instead, try speaking the dialogue aloud before writing it out. That generally isolates the stress words that occur in normal speech. The sentence can then be structured for the proper inflection.

For dialogue to be effective, you also need contrast in your characters. Their speech patterns, even the rhythm and tone of their voices, must vary. Their vocabulary must differ as well, reflecting background, education, and occupation. A simple example of diversity in dialogue would be *nuttin'*, *nothin'*, and *nothing*. The way a character talks should reveal much of himself, whether roughhewn or refined. At the same time, a character's speech must remain uniform throughout the book. To have a character say "nuttin' " on one page and "nothing" on the next destroys credibility with the reader. Never allow a character to step out of character by a lapse in his manner of speech.

The Brannocks serves as a case in point. When I wrote the novel, I foresaw the problem of drawing contrast in characters. The three Brannock brothers—Virgil, Earl, and Clint—have the same background and education. However, their occupations differ: one is a businessman, the second a gambler, and the third a lawman. Experience affects speech patterns, and I tried to draw contrasts by giving each brother his own voice. Here's a passage of dialogue that occurs early on in the book. Virgil and Earl are trying to persuade Clint to remain with them in Denver.

Clint looked from one to the other. His somber resolve turned to a slow smile. "You two sound like a couple of parrots.

58

Anybody would think you'd been rehearsing the same speech."

"Maybe so," Virgil countered. "But we're talking common, ordinary horse sense. And you know damn well it's a fact."

"He's right," Earl said emphatically. "There comes a time when a man has to take the practical outlook. You've got your own life to think about."

"Well . . . ?" Clint appeared to be wavering.

"Stay here," Virgil urged him. "We're all the family we've got now, the three of us."

Clint eyed them in silence for a time. "All right," he said in a resigned voice. "I suppose I could stick around for a while. Just so you understand it's temporary."

There are subtle shades of difference in their manner of speech. The cadence and the phrasing, an occasional choice of words, varies from one brother to the next. The way they talk, combined with the differences in temperament and physical appearance, made each of them a distinct character. By maintaining uniformity of speech throughout the book, the three brothers sounded similar but never the same. That slight distinction further enabled the reader to visualize them as individuals. They were themselves, and none of them stepped out of character.

Cussing and Foreign Words

Good dialogue must also take into account the speech patterns of people as a whole. Westerners were for the most part a salty bunch. Around women, the men might speak with a civil tongue. But among themselves, they were masters of inventive profanity. Cowhands, in particular, were renowned for their cussing ability. Which is not to say that gamblers, miners, and soldiers were any less fluent in curse words. Any man who performed rough work seasoned his speech with rough, blasphemous language. The uptown crowd, bankers and merchants, preachers and schoolteachers, were perhaps more refined. Other men, by far the majority, considered swearing a part of their routine lexicon.

To be true to the times, a Western must reflect this salty attitude. Not that every line of dialogue must necessarily turn the air blue. A great many fine Westerns have been written with hardly more than an occasional "damn." But the choice was the author's, and bordered on literary pretension. A realistic depiction of Westerners would include epithets such as "gawddamn," "Jesus Christ," and the many variants of "sonovabitch." Any complete list of swear words would in fact fill a small dictionary. Season your novels to your own tastes; but never deny a character his roots. The Old Timers cussed like hell.

Develop an ear for the way people talk. Travel the back roads and small towns and cow country barrooms. Westerners of today are better educated, but their speech still reflects their heritage. Listen for accent and cadence, the odd phrase and choice of words. People actually utter such exclamations as "I'll kiss your ass and bark like a fox!" Few writers could devise anything so expressive, or original. Engage people in conversation and play the role of a good listener. Later, jot down whatever sounds worthwhile and file it away. Some of your best dialogue, and inventive profanity, will evolve from jawboning with common folks. No course in creative writing will ever teach you that.

Nor will you learn to speak foreign languages. A great many writers, not to mention writing instructors, abhor the use of foreign words in dialogue. Yet the West of yesteryear swarmed with people who spoke broken English, or no English at all. To accurately portray such people a writer has only limited options. One method is to note in the paragraph immediately preceding the dialogue that the parties are speaking in Spanish, or Comanche, or whatever. The dialogue is then written in English, usually employing a formal, grammatically correct tone. The technique works, but to avoid sounding stilted requires a deft touch. Trying to present dialogue in broken English oftentimes sounds even worse. Either way requires lots of thought and lots of practice. Which usually means lots of rewrite.

On the other hand, I know many Western writers who flavor their dialogue with foreign words or phrases. I count myself among them, and a *gracias* here or a *hijo de puta* there often adds a dab of spice. Where it seems warranted, I have no qualms about including short passages of foreign dialogue. However, whenever I do so, I follow a strict format. The reader must somehow be informed as to the meaning of the passage, and that requires a roundabout technique. Here's the approach I used in *Bloodstorm*. Cole Braddock, the protagonist, questions a Mexican through an interpreter named Colter. Braddock speaks first.

> *"Ask him if he's had any visitors this morning."*
>
> *Colter addressed the Mexican. "Había hombres aquí hoy?"*
>
> *"Sí, señor."*
>
> *"Fueron Americanos?"*
>
> *"Sí." The Mexican nodded rapidly. "Policía Americano."*
>
> *Colter glanced at Braddock. "They've been here, all right. Allison told him they were lawmen."*

There's another method that works equally well. One character speaks in a foreign language while the other replies in English. The reader understands because the character who replies in English restates the gist of what was said in the foreign tongue. This technique should be used infrequently throughout the book, and only then for brief passages. It establishes the characters' native language, and thereafter they speak in English. Here's the approach I used in *The Stuart Women*, part of which took place in the French Quarter of New Orleans. Jovette St. Vrain, the heroine, and her sister Madeleine discuss an opera they had attended the night before. The passage has no other purpose than to add flavor to the dialogue.

> *"C'est magnifique"—Jovette laughed—"Mais ce n'est pas de l'opera."*
>
> *"What foolishness!" Madeleine replied. "You call it magnificent, yet you say it is not opera. How can that be?"*
>
> *"Because, ma petite, that cow of a soprano has transformed the entire production into a magnificent farce."*

Still another technique has to do with the brogue spoken by Irishmen. Immigrants flooded the Old West, and the Irish were to be found everywhere. The mistake commonly made by novice writers is an attempt to reproduce brogue through phonetic spelling. Instead, the writer should capture brogue through cadence and the unique juxtaposition of words. In *The Stuart Women*, the protagonist, Tom Stuart, is a steamboat captain on the Rio Grande. The passage below takes place with his rival, and the antagonist of the novel, Jack Stillman. Here's how I handled brogue.

> *Stuart threw back his head and laughed. "You're a bold one,*

Jack Stillman! And I admire a man with brass, indeed I do. But you've a ways to go before you have us licked, and there's a mortal truth if ever you heard one."

Stillman gave him a scornful look. "As I said, time's on my side, Captain Stuart. I can wait."

"Well, then, if I was you, I wouldn't hold my breath. You'll have a long wait."

The passage raises yet another bugaboo with regard to dialogue. Some academics, as well as editors in certain publishing houses, believe dialogue should follow the strictures of proper grammar. For the most part, this ivory tower crowd has never traveled west of the Hudson River. I advise you to ignore them and forget the rules of grammar when writing Western dialogue. Characters in books, like real people, are inclined to fracture the English language. In fact, your characters should dictate how they will or will not speak. One might mangle his words by saying "c'mon" and "dunno" and "figger." Another might insist on saying "come on" and "don't know" and "figure." However they talk, keep it in character. Nothing's worse than a cowhand with the diction of an erudite professor.

The Big Windy

One last pitfall with regard to dialogue. In an attempt to achieve humor, some Western writers bring together a group of characters around a campfire, or depict them lazing around a bunkhouse. Having set the stage, the writer then launches one of the characters into a variation of the "Big Windy." Otherwise known as a tall tale, this is a Western tradition that combines truth and exaggeration (or outright lies) to produce humor. The effect, when related verbally, often results in great belly laughs. When told in printed dialogue, the story requires considerable space and tends to drag on much too long. The punch line, which generally depends on a twist of some sort, rarely solicits more than a chuckle. The reader frequently completes the passage feeling it wasn't worth the effort.

Granted, a dose of humor can be employed to relieve tension in a suspenseful plot. But in writing a big windy, a writer often digs a hole so deep that it ultimately collapses. I tried it in one of my early novels,

Cimarron Jordan. The characters were gathered around the obligatory campfire and the funnyman of the crowd proceeded to spin a tall tale. The yarn went on and on, consuming almost two pages before the punch line was delivered. Later, when the book was published, I reread the scene and wished to God I hadn't written it. The big windy works well as a short story, but it's deadly dull in a novel. The better approach is to construct humorous one-liners around an everyday situation, or allow a character to drop a pithy remark. Save those tall tales to amuse your friends. They'll think you're a helluva storyteller.

Pardon a slight digression from the subject of dialogue. While we're talking about humor, let me illustrate how it works best in Westerns. Elmer Kelton, in *The Good Old Boys,* wrote a scene involving what seemed an ordinary event. Hewey Calloway took his ladylove for a ride in a wagon pulled by a team of bronc mules. There was no tipoff to the humor, even though the mules were green and ornery, still being broke to harness. Halfway through the ride, the mules "boogered" and took off across the countryside. In short order, the mules destroyed a picket fence and an outhouse, narrowly skirted a clothesline, and finally demolished the wagon itself. The wild ride, accompanied by dialogue between Hewey and his ladylove, kept me laughing through three full pages. Hell, I'm laughing even now, just thinking about it. I suggest you buy the book and read the scene for yourself. That's the way to write humor!

Who Said What

We come now to the matter of interpolations. These are the he-said-she-said bridges which identify the speaker and connect separated passages of dialogue. A great many writers add nothing to the interpolation except the appropriate pronoun, i.e., he said or she said. Other writers believe that a qualifier, usually in the form of an adverb, lends emphasis or adds tone to the speaker's voice. Still others include stage direction for the character—indicating action or thought—within the passage of dialogue. The problem arises when the writer constantly uses qualifiers, or adds too much stage direction. This tends to slow the pace and distract the reader. Dialogue should be economical, crisply stated. No wandering afield.

An example from Elmer Kelton's *The Good Old Boys* illustrates the point. Contained in a brief passage of dialogue are all the techniques just mentioned. Kelton skillfully works in a qualifier and minimal stage direction, focusing on the subject of the conversation. In the scene, Hewey Calloway pauses to inspect a weed-cutter designed and built by his nephew, Cotton. Hewey stares at the mule-drawn contraption, waiting until Cotton brings it to a halt. He appears somewhat amazed.

> *Hewey's mouth hung open.* "Boy, does that thing really work?"
>
> *Cotton made a cautious, tentative smile.* "It's no go-devil, but it cuts weeds." *The evidence lay behind him, in the row he had just finished.*
>
> *Hewey marveled at his nephew's ingenuity.* "It ain't much for pretty. Any honest-to-God farmer was to come by here, he'd die laughin'."
>
> *Cotton said defensively,* "While he's laughin', we'll be cuttin' a good clean crop of feed."

A writer has great leeway with interpolations. There are countless variations on how the bridge can be constructed and where it can be placed within a passage. Yet there are certain rules that no good writer consciously violates. Foremost is the need for clarity in dialogue. Stage directions, or descriptions of the character's actions, should be sparing rather than elaborate. Never clutter your dialogue; either discard the descriptive material or work it into the narrative. By the same token, avoid making all the characters sound alike. When that happens, they're usually speaking in *your* voice, not their own. Give every character something singular in his manner of speech.

Beware as well long passages of dialogue in which the speakers are not identified. A page of dialogue without an occasional he-said-she-said bridge inevitably leaves the reader wondering who said what. Crisp dialogue, even though it's centered between quotation marks, doesn't necessarily stand on its own. Every now and then remind the reader who's talking and provide some clue as to the tone of the conversation. In the process, learn the difference between adverbs and verbs. Here's the way it's done: "You dimwit," he said jokingly. Here's the way it's not done: "You dimwit," he chuckled. No one chuckles words, and an action verb cannot stand alone as a dialogue bridge. Should you try it, someone's liable to call you a dimwit. Stick with the proper usage.

How Not to Do It

We learn quickest by illustration. So permit me to use myself as an example. When I first began writing dialogue, I committed every error common to novice writers. All my characters talked too much and there was often an awkward quality in their manner of speech. Far worse, they all sounded alike, the cadence of their voices remarkably similar. Compounding all these faults, I wrote in elaborate stage directions which further muddied the dialogue. At the time, since I didn't know any better, it sounded brilliant. Today, I realize several good stories were flawed with inferior dialogue. Here's a prime example from my first published novel, *Black Fox.*

Let's quickly set the scene. At the outbreak of the Civil War, settlers in the north-central area of Texas were being threatened by Indian raids. Captain Buck Barry, the militia commander, requested a meeting with the leaders of the Elm Creek settlement. The scene takes place at Fort Belknap, with Allan Johnson and Grady Bragg acting as spokesmen for the settlers. The following passage of dialogue occurs halfway through the scene. Allan Johnson speaks first.

> "Captain, do I understand that you intend to order the settlers to leave their homes and occupy the fort?"
>
> "Hell yes, that's what I intend," Barry rejoined. "That's the only way I can keep you people from getting scalped." The wide grin had been replaced with a surly scowl, and all pretense of bonhomie rapidly evaporated. The mercurial transformation in his manner seemed to unsettle Allan and Grady, and they stared at him uncertainly. "You didn't seriously think I was going to ride north and engage the Comanches with twenty men?"
>
> "No, I didn't," Allan said. "But if you expect the people at Elm Creek to just walk away and leave their homes to the Indians, you're in for a shock. Sooner than do that, they'd burn 'em down themselves and move back East."
>
> "No two ways about it," Grady interjected, somewhat recovered from his awe of the officer's intimidating size. "And mister,

if you were to go over there and tell them what you just told us, they'd more'n likely laugh you all the way back to Austin."

"By Christ, that's just the kind of stubbornness that gets people killed!" Barry leaned forward, slamming his meaty paw on the desk. Startled, Allan and Grady winced slightly as the desk shuddered from the impact. "Either you move those people over here—every man, woman, and child—or goddammit, I won't be responsible for what happens to them."

Today, reading this passage, my eyes glaze. It's the work of a greenhorn writer who displayed more enthusiasm than skill. I want to sharpen a red pencil and rewrite it from start to finish. In fact, that's precisely why I selected this passage as an illustration. Having read what I have to say about dialogue, you've no doubt spotted the structural flaws in the writing. If you haven't, then I suggest you reread this chapter in its entirety. The dialogue above represents a case study in how not to do it.

Here's what I recommend. Treat the passage from *Black Fox* as an exercise in rewrite. Dissect it line by line and note the structural flaws. To make sure you've caught all the errors, you might scan the chapter again. Then, with your notes as a guide, rewrite the passage from top to bottom. Try rephrasing the dialogue itself. Extract the stage directions from the dialogue and restructure them in a more serviceable manner. Take your time and keep rewriting until you're satisfied it's right. In the process, you'll discover how much you can learn from another writer's mistakes. So I urge you to tear my dialogue apart. Learn how it's done by transforming bad to good. You'll surprise yourself.

Allow me to repeat a tenet of our craft. Dialogue is the great persuader of fiction. What your characters say and how they say it convinces the reader that illusion is truth. There's no mystical secret to writing good dialogue, no hard and fast rules. Nor is there a simple way to master the unique sounds of Western vernacular. You instruct yourself in these things by talking to people and reading the works of other craftsmen. Then, finally, you give voice to your own characters. You listen while they talk. You persuade the reader through their words.

All actors, of course, need a stage. For your characters to play their roles and speak their lines, you'll have to create yet another illusion.

The scenery and props, all the accoutrements of stagecraft, must be put into place. But to pull it off you need something that borders on the spectral. The smoke and mirrors of fiction.

You need a narrator.

BIG KNIFE R.
HEART R.
CANNON BALL
BOX ELDER
LITTLE MISSOURI R.
GRAND R.
D
CHERRY R.
Crow Cr.
ELLE FOURCHE OR BIG CHEYENNE RIVER
OAK
PINE CR.
CLEAR WATER
BEAR BUTTE
Bear Cr.
AN KAKA
BLACK HILLS
BOX ELDER
HARNEYS PEAK
SPRING C
RAPID
ELK
MAUVAIS TERR
HAT CR.
Corn Cr.
Porcupine Cr.
Porcupine Tail
MANS FK.

5. The Narrator's Voice

arrative defies simple definition. The dictionary defines it as the process of telling a story. Yet storytelling relates events, depicts action, and moves characters from here to there. So we must ultimately conclude that narration involves a complex of factors. However, within that complex, there's a key word. Action!

Nothing happens without it. Characters are immobile, their lines unspoken, until someone infuses them with life. Events are frozen in time, waiting for someone to set them in motion. Time itself stands still, space and sound imprisoned, until someone puts the clock running. All that requires action, the release of energy. Someone to energize the narrative. A narrator.

Early on, then, a writer must decide who will narrate his story. The traditional choices are first-person narrator and third-person narrator. The former is an actual character in the book, telling the story as he lives it. The latter is the unseen author, relating the story in an offstage voice. There are few similarities between these two forms of narration, or viewpoint, and the writer must weigh them carefully. Their marked differences make the decision one of considerable importance.

Onstage Voice

Let's begin with first-person narrator. As a normal practice, most Western writers select the protagonist as the narrator. The principal reason is that the first-person narrator is onstage throughout the entire book. Everything that happens is related from his point of view. As the narrator, speaking in first person, he says "I did this" and "I saw that." He observes every event that takes place and he describes the actions of every character, including his own. Nothing can happen unless he's on the spot, there to report it.

Of course, one of the other principal characters can be selected as the narrator. Doing so imposes certain restrictions on the story line as well as the writer. The character/narrator must now be present when the lead character, the protagonist, does anything of consequence. That can create awkward situations wherein the character/narrator just happens to be on the scene whenever something important transpires. A skilled writer can usually make it seem credible rather than glaringly coincidental. Done poorly, it can take on comedic aspects that were never intended.

A great many beginning writers are drawn to the first-person narrative. It's the most direct method of telling a story, simpler than the third-person format. By extension, the narrator is speaking for the writer, and their voices tend to meld into one. Moreover, the narrator becomes a fixed reference point around which characters and events revolve. There's an element of control in all this that seems irresistible to some writers. To use a Western metaphor, it's a one-horse buggy, with a single set of reins, as compared with the six-horse hitch of a stagecoach. Driving it, particularly for the new writer, appears to be easier.

The chief danger is that the writer may put too much of himself into the narrator. He then becomes a ventriloquist, rather than creating a character and allowing the character to narrate the story in his own voice. The principal advantage is that first-person makes the reader a participant in unfolding events. Everything the narrator relates seems personalized and there's an air of immediacy to the story. The reader feels involved, a sort of you-were-there sensation. For some people, it's almost real.

Whatever the advantages, first person does have its limitations. Foremost is the fact that it locks the writer into one character's mind. The narrator must think a certain way, speak in a certain idiom, and relate events in a certain tone of voice. All rolled into one, he is an active participant, a not altogether impartial observer, and a chronicler of what's happening around him. To compound the problem, all these things must remain consistent throughout the entire book. One minor deviation will destroy the narrator's credibility and thereby dilute the impact of the story. In other words, the writer must step into character and stay there. He has now become writer/character/narrator.

There's more. To pull it off, the writer has to create a narrator with a compelling personality. The reader has to listen to this character page after page, the length of the book. Unless the narrator is interesting and likeable and a helluva storyteller, the reader simply won't tag along. Because the narrator is constantly onstage, the writer will feel tempted to adorn him with offbeat mannerisms and ear-catching jargon. The temptation must be suppressed, or at the very least tempered. A distinctive voice and a compelling personality have nothing to do with tricky adornments. That's the easy way out, and a lazy writer's refuge. Create, instead, a narrator who will last over the long haul. A one-of-a-kind without the clown costume.

Still another drawback with first-person narrative is getting inside the narrator's head. The reader must come to know this character intimately, share his thoughts and emotions. That requires stopping the action, permitting the narrator to ponder and reflect and express his own feelings. The way it's done is with the inner monologue, a passage in which the narrator talks to himself. But revealing the inner workings of a narrator's mind must be done with discretion, and quickly. Unless his thoughts bear directly on the story, the reader will begin to squirm. Philosophy and abstraction slow the pace and make for soggy reading. By all means allow the narrator to reveal something of the inner man. Just do it fast and do it neat. Then get back to the action.

First-Person Bugaboos

On to the next problem. How does the first-person narrator describe himself? He can hardly step out of character to list his own attributes. For the narrator to say "I'm tall and sledge-shouldered and lightning-fast with a gun" would border on the absurd. The solution is to let the other characters describe the narrator. In dialogue, they can refer to his physical appearance, his personality traits, and his assorted skills. To be most effective, these revelations should be made over a span of time and by more than one character. Too much, too quickly makes it obvious that the reader is being provided with information. Another device is to let the narrator's reaction to events and people reveal something of himself. However, it must be underplayed, done with subtlety. Nobody likes a narrator who toots his own horn.

Nor should the writer sound any trumpets. With a first-person narrator, some writers feel a compulsion to air their personal views. They create a narrator who spouts soapbox diatribes and drifts off into inner monologues that express some partisan bias. Certain writers turn their novels into revisionist history, distorting actual historical events to vent their own anger or beliefs. Others dwell on intolerance, injustice, and a long laundry list of social issues. Few readers will suffer through Western novels written to espouse a slanted viewpoint. Even fewer editors will publish thinly disguised polemics. A novelist, however well intentioned, has no business rewriting history.

A final problem has to do with offstage events. Things happen in a story that cannot be portrayed directly. Space limitations dictate that *all* the events, however important to the plot, cannot be witnessed by the first-person narrator. Logic dictates that certain events in any story *would not* take place within sight of the narrator. To skirt the problem, the writer must somehow depict such events in an oblique manner. One method is to let other characters reveal the information in dialogue. Of course, the dialogue has to be addressed to the narrator, or at least within his earshot. Another device is to let the narrator reflect on something he's been told or overheard or read in the newspaper. His inner ruminations then reveal the information to the reader. Here again, the reader must perceive it as part of the story, rather than a contrived device to pass along information. In effect, it's a magic act that relies on misdirection. The writer openly presents one thing while deftly slipping another from his sleeve. Call it literary legerdemain.

By now you've probably gathered that I'm not an advocate of first-person narrative. In the course of thirty-one novels, I've never considered using first person. The limitations, in my opinion, outweigh the advantages by a wide margin. While it's simpler to write, first person has built-in pitfalls that can trap any writer. Perhaps the greatest of the lot is sustaining a constant onstage narrator while at the same time keeping him involved in interesting and suspenseful action. Too often such novels are padded with dull-as-dirt dialogue and long passages of inner monologue. The narrator comes off as a dullard, with nothing worth saying and no story to tell.

On the other hand, many excellent Westerns have been written in first person. The narrator is an absorbing character as well as an acute observer of events and other characters. The plot is detailed but swift-paced, thoroughly engrossing. Dialogue is sharp, true to the ear, and bears directly on either revelation of character or the story. Inner monologues by the narrator are both compelling and challenging, filled with thoughts designed to provoke a response or advance the story line. There's no lost motion, no slow-as-molasses scenes, no padding simply to make the book longer. These are good novels because the advantages of first person are stressed and the limitations are overcome. Writers who favor first person would do equally well in third person. They are craftsmen who take pride in their work.

Jack Schaefer is one such writer. His novel *Shane* employed a first-person narrator. Further complicating his task, he selected as his narrator a young boy named Bob. The story was serious in nature, involving bloodshed and death, and profound injustice. There were subplots revolving around Shane and other characters, principally the boy's parents. Yet the story was told from Bob's point of view, and told so skillfully that the reader was seldom aware of the narrator's age. Other works by Schaefer have been written in third person, and they were written with equal skill. He's a master storyteller, one of the great craftsmen in the Western field. Few writers possess his ability to skip back and forth between first-person and third-person narrative. It's a literary high-wire act of considerable daring.

Offstage Voice

About now, you're probably wondering why I'm such a hard-and-fast proponent of third-person narrative. Every writer has preferences, and you might easily conclude that my reasons are a matter of personal taste rather than objective analysis. So let me suggest a question that has far more relevance than my own opinion. Why are the vast majority of novels written in third person? To narrow it further, why are most Westerns written in third person?

Let's take the question still another step. Third-person narration requires that the writer state it in terms of "He entered the saloon." As mentioned earlier, it's considerably easier to use the first-person format of "I entered the saloon." To underscore the point, presenting it in third person increases the difficulty for the writer. So why do most writers opt for third person and therefore make their lives harder?

The answer begins with the fact that third-person narration allows the writer an omniscient viewpoint. An offstage voice, heard but never seen, the writer becomes an unnamed narrator. He is omnipresent—everywhere at the same time—on the scene whenever *anything* happens in the story. He sees from the point of view of every character and therefore he sees all things. Like God, he's on the spot wherever a sparrow falls.

From this omniscient vantage point, the writer enjoys almost total freedom. He can plumb the mind of any character, explore emotions and motivations. Characters speak for themselves and live their own lives, but always under the writer's direction. He orchestrates their actions and conversations, their reflections and thoughts. Then he records it all in an offstage voice.

Yet the writer/narrator can also speak in his own voice. As an example, he can provide the necessary background for a scene, a sort of color commentary. Or he can supply needed information to the reader, presenting it in the form of objective observations. He can relate what's happened in the past, or an incident that has occurred between scenes, reported but never actually shown. He can tell the reader anything at any time in the narrative, even momentarily interrupting dialogue to provide a salient detail or added background. And because of his omniscient position, he has no limitations with regard to time frame or subject. He knows all, past or present.

Still in his own voice, the third-person narrator can describe a scene as it happens. He has the liberty to portray action, present conflict, and relate the elements that build suspense. There is no need for modesty, as with the first-person narrator. The writer/narrator can render the physical description of a character with complete anonymity. He can remark on mannerisms, probe sentiment, and convey the impressions one character makes on another. There is nothing he cannot relate or describe or observe. His omniscience, that offstage voice, allows him to say whatever he pleases. Whenever he chooses to say it.

Plotting for third-person narrative becomes somewhat more complicated. All the characters now have their own viewpoint, which opens a whole new world of possibilities. To illustrate, the plot could be constructed in such a way that the viewpoint shifts from character to character, scene by scene. Nonetheless, most experienced Western writers avoid complex plot structures. They center their novels instead on the protagonist, the lead character. The hero appears in virtually every scene, and the other characters swirl around him as the story unfolds. Occasionally, a scene may be told from the viewpoint of the villain or another principal character. But the majority of Westerns keep it relatively simple by reserving stage center for the protagonist.

All of which raises the question of subplots. Here again, the majority of Westerns are relatively straightforward, with perhaps one subplot. In most instances, the protagonist is also involved in this peripheral story, which simplifies it even further. Another major character can be introduced and that character's story can be told without overcomplicating things. Since the subplot invariably merges with the main plot, the writer adds nuance while still maintaining tight control. The third-person narrator sometimes shifts point of view between the protagonist and the other principal character in those scenes involving the subplot. Yet the spotlight, for all practical purposes, remains on the hero.

The first three novels I sold followed this format. While I had no formal training in writing, I somehow recognized the inherent danger of piling complexity upon complexity. Instinct also warned me against peopling these novels with a large cast of principal characters. In third-person narration, the introduction of several primary characters adds greatly to the writer's burden. First, for the plot to work, all these characters must be periodically trotted out and given their moment onstage. Worse yet, the third-person narrator must now deal in multiple points of view. Clearly, a primary character ceases to play a major role unless his perspective of things is somehow depicted. So the writer/narrator has no option but to delve into the minds of all these people. Failing that, they will never become fully realized characters.

Multiviewpoint Stories

There is still another hazard unique to third-person narration. Writers are forever tempted to tell the stories of several primary characters within the framework of one book. To pull it off, all these stories must somehow intermesh and ultimately converge into the main plot. The complexity snowballs, however, when the third-person narrator becomes ensnarled in multiviewpoint stories. Now it's no longer a matter of delving into the minds of these people and exploring their relationship with a single protagonist. For they are all protagonists, even though one character may assume a degree of dominance. Their separate stories must be told, and whenever one of them walks onstage, the narrator must conform to that character's distinct viewpoint. In this instance, the writer/narrator might be likened to a stage director presenting a story within a story within a story. Things tend to get hectic the minute the curtain rises.

A writer needs loads of experience before attempting such a tour de force. In dealing with diverse personalities and multiviewpoint stories, there's a real danger the book will have a splintered effect that never quite comes together at the end. I resisted the temptation until my tenth novel, *The Kincaids*. This was a multigeneration family saga which told the story of the settlement of Oklahoma. The time span was 1871-1924, and included in the broader picture were the stories of the railroads, the Five Civilized Tribes, the outlaw gangs, and the birth of the oil industry. The length of the novel was 508 pages, the longest I've ever written.

Jerrold Mundis, my mentor at the time, considered the project much too ambitious. The concept intrigued him, and he believed it would make a superb story. But he felt I shouldn't attempt it until I had another eight or ten books under my belt. Heedless of his advice, I waded into what quickly became a monumental undertaking. The scope of the book, encompassing a half dozen primary characters and multiviewpoint stories, threatened to swamp me at every turn. Stubbornness, as much as determination, enabled me to complete the project in a few days shy of one year. The Western Writers of America awarded *The Kincaids* the Golden Spur for Best Western Historical Novel of 1976. Still, in reflective moments, I sometimes wish I had followed my mentor's advice. *The Kincaids* would have been a better book for it.

Hindsight nonetheless taught me a lesson. Of the next seventeen novels I wrote, only three involved multiviewpoint stories. I waited until the twenty-eighth novel, *The Brannocks*, before attempting another project of such breadth and scope. This time, however, I structured the story into four books, and wrote them over a period of two years. Their total length approached 1400 pages, covering a time span of 1865-1887. Older now, and somewhat more objective about my work, I believe these novels fulfilled the greater part of their potential. The members of the Brannock family, and other primary characters, were more fully realized than those in *The Kincaids*. The reason for that improvement boils down quite simply to experience. A writer matures at his craft by learning from his mistakes.

Let's suppose you aspire to write multiviewpoint stories. Those sprawling, panoramic sagas spread over a large and colorful canvas. I know a couple of Western writers, both of them gifted with enormous talent, whose first novels involved stories within stories. Their books were widely successful, originally printed in hardcover and later reprinted in paperback. But of all the writers I know, only these two fit into that category. The others, in the main, would never attempt such an ambitious project. They are content to write traditional Westerns with a single protagonist and a straightforward story line. The remainder, and they're few in number, undertook multiviewpoint novels only after years of perfecting their craft. So allow me to offer some advice distilled from the experience of writers I've met along the way. When you're starting out, write three or four novels wherein characters and events revolve around a single protagonist. Having mastered that format, you might then consider a work of greater complexity. Or then again, maybe you won't.

Some writers find their métier and stick with it for a lifetime. They prefer the smaller book, the limited viewpoint, the enclosed story. Others feel the need to stretch themselves as writers, constantly experimenting with new forms and uncharted complexities. Neither group has the universal answer to what's best for all writers. They've determined only what's best for them, just as you will one day decide who you are as a writer. A similar rule prevails with regard to first-person narrative or third-person narrative. You may prefer one over the other, to hell with limitation or freedom, simplicity or complexity. Through trial and error, you may discover you're comfortable with either format. No one can say yea or nay to whatever you do, for the decision represents a matter of personal choice. In the end, that's what makes horse races.

And writers, too.

Details Through Exposition

Exposition can be defined as information. The information a reader requires to know all he needs to know about the characters and the situation. Narrative advances the story line; exposition provides background details and establishes reasons for what occurs. To adequately present exposition, the writer must therefore know how the plot will develop and what will happen in the ultimate climax. Any confusion in the writer's mind would surface in the exposition and inevitably muddle the story beyond comprehension. As a result, the information presented in exposition must be relevant to the action that ensues. Irrelevant information, providing details that have no direct bearing on character or situation, forces the reader to sift what's important from what's not. Complexity works only when it serves to strengthen the story. Otherwise it's a form of literary pretension.

Done well, exposition informs the reader as to the causes behind the characters' actions and their evolving conflicts. Of course, for greatest effect, what the reader learns in the exposition must later be shown through dramatic events. Don't just tell the reader that the antagonist is a sinister coldblooded brute. Show the antagonist involved in an act of sinister, coldblooded brutality. Dramatic impact, which requires making it credible, results from depicting rather than telling. Finally, for the exposition to achieve force, an element of instability must be introduced. The characters must be thrown into conflict with themselves, with each other, and with the situation. That sense of jeopardy further heightens the experience for the reader. It's the end product of good exposition.

Of course, there are times when exposition has no other purpose than to provide information. Westerns have perhaps more need of exposition than genres such as mystery and romance. How a roundup was conducted, or the way a mountain man trapped beaver, requires that the reader be provided with unfamiliar details. To leave out such details would dilute the story and deny it an authentic flavor. On the other hand, the writer must present the detail within the context of the story line. Otherwise the reader has the impression he's being force-fed information. Elmer Kelton turned the trick with great aplomb in *The Good Old Boys*. He wrote a scene in which the protagonist, Hewey Calloway, was treating cattle for screwworm. The details, provided for all those noncowboy readers, were dovetailed into the midst of the scene. Here's the way the information was presented.

> *The screwworm fly thrived in warm and humid weather. It was attracted to any scrape or cut that brought warm blood to the surface. This could be a man-made wound such as a castration cut or a peeling brand. It could be accidental, from running against a rough tree or a barbed-wire fence, or horn gouges incurred in fighting. It could be natural. In newly born calves the flies attacked the bleeding navel and set death's time clock to work in the very same place where the umbilical cord had given*

78

life. The flies laid their eggs, which soon expanded into a wrig-
gling white mass of flesh-eating screw-shaped worms that gorged
themselves and drew more flies and grew in numbers until death
put an end to the animal's torment.

Kelton presented the information as the third-person narrator. The way
he presented it underscores a critical point. Exposition must be written
in an interesting manner, structured to hold the reader's interest while
at the same time informing him. Let's face it, the subject of screwworms
doesn't interest a helluva lot of people apart from cattlemen. Yet Kelton
provided the details in a way that has about it a sense of life-and-death
immediacy. Before the scene ends, the reader understands that treating
cows for screwworm is a dirty, thoroughly unpleasant job. Nonetheless,
it's a task cowhands perform to stave off the loss of money-on-the-hoof.
That's exposition at its best, rendered in a way that interests and informs and relates directly to the story. The reader finished the scene
with a finer appreciation for Hewey Calloway's workday chores.

Tricks and Techniques

A word to the aspiring writer. In the past, you read novels for the enjoy-
ment of reading. But now, with an urge to write books of your own, you
must look upon reading as a learning process. Your principal concern
should be discovering what constitutes a good novel. What makes it
work.

To begin, select the books of several different writers, established
names in the Western field. Expose yourself to a synthesis of the genre
by picking novels from various categories, traditional as well as historical. While you're reading, look for the variations of plot and theme being
played out against a Western backdrop. Your object is to learn how the
story was tailored to the criteria of a particular genre.

Teach yourself to read like a writer. That involves a more deliberate
pace, one which allows you to analyze as you read. Take the novel apart,
determine exactly how it's structured. Keep asking yourself *what* the
writer's doing and *how* he's doing it. Another revealing question is *why*
the characters do what they do. That often provides a tipoff as to how the
writer plotted the story or structured a certain scene. When you're
stumped, stop and reread it. Study it until you understand how the writer achieved a particular effect.

No book on the craft of writing can teach you all the tricks. You must come to the point where you look upon reading as an educational process. A novel that keeps you turning pages represents a manual on plot and pace, character and dialogue. Approach it from an analytical standpoint and every book you read will reveal some new aspect of technique. Eventually you'll learn to distinguish what works from what doesn't work. In time, you will have collected a whole bag of tricks, each one worth the reading of an entire novel. Your own work will benefit immensely from the experience.

Technique is no substitute for genius. But technique, once mastered, can transform a writer of modest talent into an author of impressive credentials. Nowhere does the thought apply more directly than in your choice of a narrator. First-person narration and third-person narration have little in common apart from telling a story. A beginning writer who flits between the two formats may never master either. Instead, you should begin by selecting the format that most appeals to you as a reader. You're already comfortable with it, and as a result, the technique will come easier. Whether first person or third person, write at least two or three novels in that format. Then, if you're the adventurous sort, you can always experiment with the other method. The point here is that not everyone has the flexibility to function as a jack-of-all-trades. Determine what you do best and master it.

Odds 'n Ends

A writer can seldom indulge in long passages of narrative. The typical reader prefers scenes strung together with a minimum of narrative. Work the description into your scene, a bit here, a bit there. Work important points of research into the story casually, never in an obvious manner. The reader will skip past large chunks of information.

Sculpture every page. Write short paragraphs, varied in length, and interspersed with dialogue. Avoid paragraphs that stand like monoliths, defying understanding or conquest. Few people read them, so why bother to write them? It's just that simple.

Bad writing is loads of fun. It stems from an old adage: Ignorance is bliss. Anyone ignorant of the rules of good writing can have a whale of a time churning out turgid, overblown prose. Sometimes the end product will even be bought and published. Editors make mistakes, too.

Good writing is hard work. Laborious and exacting, it demands adherence to tough, unyielding strictures. After my mentor taught me the rules of good writing, I experienced a change in attitude. No longer would conscience allow me to do it the wrong way. Never more earnest, I told him: "You've taken all the fun out of writing." Yet it was an equitable exchange, fun for fulfillment. Pride of craft replaced the giddy freedom of sloppy prose.

The secret of good writing is to construct powerful, well-organized sentences. Your choice of words, and the way those words are interlocked, should excite and intrigue the reader. Until a sentence says precisely what you mean it to say, until the cadence rings true, then you are obliged to rewrite and rewrite. And if necessary, rewrite it yet again.

On occasion people will ask me, "How's the writing going?" I have a standard response: "A sentence at a time." For those who are nonwriters, the answer invariably solicits a chuckle. Writers, on the other hand, take it as a sober statement of fact. They know that a novel is constructed one sentence at a time. They know as well that it's no laughing matter. Sentences are damn serious business.

An anonymous writer once reduced the craft of writing to a single sentence. He said: "The presentation of agony is best served by the simplest truth." Perhaps he meant that an understated scene is better than an overwritten scene. Or that the risk of leaving something unsaid is far preferable to redundancy. Certainly, he meant that narration must be written in crisp prose, devoid of flowery language and three-dollar words. All the more, he was stating that a narrator must never deal in sensational reporting or sloppy sentimentality. While sentiment has its place in fiction, sentimentality marks the amateur writer who forces his narrator to speak like a sophomoric dolt. So there you have it. *The presentation of agony is best served by the simplest truth.* In eleven words, that says more about the craft of writing than many books on the subject. When you write your next novel, keep those eleven words uppermost in mind. You'll never find a better motto.

Nor will you find a motto more difficult to follow. The writer quoted above spoke with eloquence and precision. His intent was to create a single sentence that would encompass every facet of a complex discipline. Further, he intended that the axiom should withstand the test of time. He wanted what he said to be remembered by how he said it. In effect, he was demonstrating that most elusive aspect of the writing profession. He said it with style.

So the motto has yet another meaning. Those eleven words allude to a literary enigma. Writers throughout time have discussed it and dissected it and attempted to explain it. Of course, their greater effort lay in the search to find it for themselves. To attain, at last, the thing called style.

A voice all their own.

MISSOURI RIVER
SIOUX RES.
DACOTA R.
Frozen Man
Hole Cr.
Old Ft Pierre
Ft SULLY
Cedar Cr.
Elm Cr
Old Ft. George
MEDICINE HILL
INDIAN VILLAGE
Winnebago Reserve
Chanke
White
Medicine Cr.
American Crow
Red Cedar Cr.
Bad Land
South Fork
Oak Cr.
Two Tail
Dog Ears
Water Hole
Wetstone
Scalp Cr.
YANKTON
RESERVATION
KEYA PAYA R.
Ft RANDAL
PONKA R.
RASKA
ELKH
CALAMAS R.
BEAVER
Dismal R.
NORTH BRANCH
PAWN
RES.
LOUP
Grand Island Station
PLATTS
STATION
SOUTH BRANCH
UNION
WOOD RIVER
Kearney Station
Station
FT. McPHER
FLAT RIVER
GRAND I

6.
Craft Your
Own Voice

To develop style you must find your natural writing voice. Style is not cleverly urbane writing or revolutionary prose rhythms. Style is simply the *way* you write. Yet there is nothing simple about it. Nor is it easily defined.

Some writers consciously contrive a style. Others are purposely imitative, aping the style of writers they admire. The truly gifted display a singular style from the outset. For most of us, however, the search for style seems never ending. We find our unique "voice" only by writing and writing and writing. Our search constitutes a form of on-the-job training.

Too often, beginning writers concentrate on style at the expense of plot. Either they've read articles or heard discussions on the style of such novelists as Faulkner and Hemingway. These learned dissertations invariably dwell on the style of the writing rather than the substance of the novel. The newcomer mistakenly draws the conclusion that style is substance, that the novel succeeds only because of style. What he fails to grasp is that all great novelists were storytellers first and stylists by way of framing words in their own voice. Style emerges when a writer focuses on story rather than literary affectations.

John Huston, the director and writer, once said: "There is so much talk of style and technique, of my 'unifying technique,' of a Huston scene. I've always been fascinated to know what it was. I myself haven't the vaguest idea." Huston's remarks went to the very heart of the matter. Superb storytellers, whether on film or in novels, are frequently unaware that they possess a distinct style. Those who do recognize the style in their work are often aware of it only after the fact. When they began, they were searching for their style, as do all writers. For the most part, however, they were not consciously attempting to *devise* a style.

Anyone who seeks to contrive a style will inevitably write novels that sound contrived. Distinctive writing evolves naturally, and as with John Huston, you'll know you have it when someone comments on your "style." Until then you keep searching.

The most commonly recognized styles are the *lean* and the *overwritten*. Lean style can be identified by economical sentence structure and the absence of descriptive words. Overwritten style relies on a barrage of adjectives and florid, oftentimes emotional, descriptive passages. Somewhere in between lies the balanced style that most writers strive to attain. Neither lean nor overwritten, the prose advances the story in an unobtrusive manner. The reader becomes involved with character and story, not style.

Let me illustrate with samples of my own work. Here's a passage from *Black Fox*, the first novel I had published. The overwritten style speaks for itself.

> *The Irishman's breathing was labored and shallow, and a dark, crimson blotch covered his chest. Working feverishly, the black man ripped his shirt open and stared sickenly as a small, neat hole beneath the breastbone pumped a bright fountain of blood. Tearing a strip from the shirt, he jammed it against the wound, trying desperately to staunch the bubbling hole.*

Twenty-eight novels later, I wrote a similar passage in *Windward West*. Here again, it involves one man watching another man die. The style indicates a degree of control.

> *A quicksilver splinter of time slipped past and Earl's eyes went blank. His mouth opened in a death rattle and his hand dropped to the ground. He stared upward at nothing.*
> *Clint leaned forward and gently closed his eyes.*

There is a marked difference in style between the two novels. *Black Fox* was larded with adjectives and florid prose. *Windward West* was spare, though not lean, with tighter sentence structure. Anyone reading the books today would question that they were written by the same writer. Which serves to illustrate a point made earlier.

The search for style usually takes time. A beginning writer often demonstrates undisciplined enthusiasm. His choice of words, and how he structures those words into sentences, shows little restraint. Characters stare "sickenly" and blood pumps in "a bright fountain." There is a tendency to overstate it, as though writing everything in *italics*. Those punchy words, the adjectives and adverbs, are here, there, and everywhere. Hardly anything is left to the reader's imagination.

The experienced writer restrains himself. He knows that adjectives, like red pepper, should be used sparingly. Time has taught him that a dramatic event requires no hype. Instead, he allows the event to state its own case, and natural drama follows. He keeps things tight and controlled, striving always for balance. Whatever must be said he says, and stops. He permits the reader to imagine the rest.

Yet knowing when to stop isn't all that simple. A major problem for beginning writers has to do with redundancy. Saying it once doesn't seem to make the point with sufficient impact. So they say it again, and perhaps again, expressing the same thought in different words. What merits a single sentence blossoms into a redundant paragraph. Or maybe the original thought is presented some pages later, reworded but nonetheless repetitious. For the reader, it's tiresome and something of an insult. No one should be told the same thing over and over again. Say it once and say it well. Then stop.

Still another trap has to do with polysyllabic words. Searching for style, the beginning writer often becomes enamored with highfalutin language. Let's call them three-dollar words, the jawbusters and tongue twisters. A writer usually stumbles across them while pursuing synonyms in the thesaurus. Inexperience leads him to believe that fancy words—the bigger, the better—will lend style to his writing. Instead, it confuses the story and leaves the reader thumbing through a dictionary. Such words are anathema to style. Now, substitute "a curse" for "anathema." Either serves, but the ten-cent word serves best.

Back to the Basics

Technique and *style* are often considered synonymous. Let's separate the two words and define *technique* as a method of employing certain basic skills. By that definition, technique can further your efforts to craft your own voice. Certain fundamental rules combine to form technique, whether it's playing a piano or writing a novel. Your understanding of those rules, and their practical application, are essential to the development of style. Ignore them, and your search for style will be conducted in the dark. Follow them, and your path will be illuminated however far you travel. Here are some thoughts on technique, gleaned from my own experience as well as my association with other writers. In retrospect, we all arrived at the same conclusion. Our search for style began with the basics.

There is no substitute for a command of the English language. All writing begins with the use of words, and good writing employs each word with precision. Webster's defines *syntax* as the organization and relationship of word groups, phrases, clauses, and sentences; sentence structure. For writers, the proper application of syntax denotes professionalism and pride of craft. A mastery of syntax leads like a flagstone pathway to the origin of style. Once you have a command of the language, you have the power of expression, the ability to communicate. How well you communicate will in large part define your style.

Unless you've mastered the language, don't expect a warm reception in the world of publishing. Editors cringe at grammatical errors and unimaginative prose, all of which undermine good storytelling. The telltale signs are easy to spot, for the whole thing abounds with clichés and slipshod sentence construction. Quickly, one fault compounding another, the characters become wooden stereotypes and the narrative takes on a leaden quality. The end result tags the author as an amateur, or perhaps a careless hack. Avoid either of those labels by strict attention to grammar and syntax. If necessary, undertake a self-education program, or enroll in a night school. To repeat, there's no substitute for a command of the language. You must have it.

Conversely, there are times when proper grammar doesn't work in a novel. A writer who adheres unwaveringly to the rules often produces stilted prose. Worse, his characters tend to talk like a highbrow English teacher. Of course, you have to know the rules before you'll recognize where it's possible to break them. In my own writing, I frequently drop a comma to produce the desired rhythm in a sentence. On occasion, to underscore a thought, I end a paragraph with an incomplete sentence. Yet I'm aware of the rule being broken, and it's not done in a haphazard manner. Instead, I purposely break it to achieve a certain effect, and that's permissible. Some of the world's great novelists bent the rules out of shape when it served their purpose. The critics raved about their "style."

The Three Cs of writing are *crisp, clear,* and *concise.* Crisp means it expresses the thought in sharp, clean-cut language. Clear requires that it be stated in simple, comprehensible terms. Concise demands that it be succinct, short and to the point. These three elements are basic to any good writing, whether it be business correspondence or Western novels. An abstruse sentence that runs on and on, expressing thought after thought, employing arcane words and abstract language, tying everything together with commas and semicolons, all too often requires the mind of a cryptanalyst to decipher the meaning. You've just finished reading a sentence that illustrates the point. Whenever you have to read something twice to get the drift, you know it has to be rewritten. Stick with crisp, clear, and concise. Your style will improve right there. On the spot.

Everyone knows that correct spelling is basic to good writing. Or do they? Editors constantly complain about the spelling errors in manuscripts. Ordinary words, the ones used in daily conversation, are misspelled just as frequently as the three-dollar words. A mistake here and there might be a typo; consistent misspelling signifies an author who either doesn't know any better or simply can't be bothered. An established writer, one with a proven track record, might get by with sloppy spelling. His editor may choose to overlook the errors and leave the corrections to a copyeditor. A beginning writer will rarely be treated with such indulgence. Irked by spelling errors, the editor may feel it's just not worth the trouble. The manuscript would then be returned without having been read. You therefore have incentive to hit the dictionary and correct your own spelling. Who cares about style when it's buried in an avalanche of misspelled words? An editor won't, that's for damn sure.

The thesaurus represents an invaluable writing tool. Mark Twain, who first gained prominence with his Western stories, once observed: "The difference between the right word and the almost right word is the difference between lightning and the lightning bug." What he meant was that a writer must become both a student and a collector of words. The right word, as opposed to any old word that comes to mind, results in a polished sentence. In the end, those polished sentences will in large measure determine your style. After all, how you word it and the way you word it would serve as a definition of style. Unless your thesaurus is tattered and dog-eared, you're not searching hard enough or long enough for the right word. Nor will your search for style make significant progress. Give the reader sentences that pop and sizzle with *lightning*. You'll find it in the thesaurus.

Getting from Here to There

Lots of writers have trouble with transitions. Briefly, a transition can be defined as the bridge connecting one passage of narrative with another. An example would be the smooth movement from one scene to the next, or from chapter to chapter. The best transitions are quick and neat, without any long, involved explanations. Let's suppose there is a time lapse between scenes, and your character has to appear in a different location when the new scene opens. The simplest solution would be to skip four spaces and resume the story at the new time and new place. Given the bare facts, the reader will figure out for himself that a time lapse has occurred. Getting characters onstage and off within a scene is somewhat more complicated. You can manage it easily enough with dialogue and brief explanatory passages to cover entrance and exit. Study the work of other writers, analyze the multitude of techniques they use to shift time and place. How well you handle transitions will have a major effect on your style. You have to get from here to there with agility.

Flashbacks are an altogether different type of transition. Essentially, you're switching back and forth in time, moving from the present to the past. Unless it's handled with skill, you risk losing the reader when you turn back the clock. The trick is to clue the reader that a switch has occurred without an elaborate explanation. The techniques for pulling off a flashback are many and varied. Almost all of them involve ending a scene with a character reflecting on some past incident. An alternative has the third-person narrator provide the clue by looking backward in time. The break from present to past can then be accomplished by skipping four spaces and going immediately into the flashback scene. Another method is to end the chapter as just described and then open the next chapter with the flashback. I've written only one novel (my sixth) in which I made extensive use of flashbacks. The experience left me convinced that one or two flashbacks per novel are more than enough. Too many leaps back and forth make the reader wonder whether the major story line is set in the present or the past. Nonetheless, there are many fine novelists who enhance their style by mastering flashbacks. You may be one of them.

Clarity and Clichés

Clarity in writing cannot be divorced from style. Ambiguity being the opposite of clarity, it follows that style suffers when a writer uses imprecise language. Should you become bogged down in a sentence, it's generally because you've constructed something too involved. The sentence needs to be broken apart and restructured, stated another way. Stop and ask yourself: What am I trying to say? Forget how you just said it and reduce the thought to the simplest possible terms. Pare it to the bare bones. Viewed in that form, the essence of the thought quickly becomes apparent. Turn it around and upside down until you understand precisely what it is you're trying to express. You will then find a way to say it with clarity, and style.

Nothing undermines style more than the use of clichés. The trite, shopworn phrase is the trademark of a lazy writer. No innovation or originality is required when a writer relies upon clichés. Simply grab any old chestnut and put it down on paper. Faster, less thought involved, and far easier. Style be damned!

Clichés are also insidious. They creep into our work with no conscious awareness. A writer gets stuck in a narrative passage and suddenly a moth-eaten phrase emerges from the typewriter. At the moment, it sounds good and perfectly conveys the meaning intended. Yet, where style is concerned, there's a hitch. It stinks.

Nor is there any limitation on clichés. Every aspect of writing remains vulnerable to the stale and the overworked. As a genre, the Western has bromides to spare. How many times have you read about a "blood-red sunset"? Or the "steely-eyed" gunman with "nerves of ice"? Narrative and physical description are particularly susceptible to the hackneyed phrase. Style too often suffers from the easy way out.

Dialogue presents a somewhat different problem. You should always try to revamp a cliché and state it in an original manner. However, bear in mind, you're not writing high art. Western vernacular is loaded with clichés that ring true to the time and place. When one character says to another, "Fish or cut bait," you'll be hard pressed to improve on it. Of course, you shouldn't allow *all* your characters to spout bromides *all* the time. A cliché here and there serves to season dialogue. Too many old saws becomes a style in itself. A style to be avoided.

Words and Images

Simile and metaphor are often confused by the beginning writer. One draws a direct comparison while the other creates an image. They are both integral to crafting your own style. How well you use them affects the reader's perception of your "voice." Let's first define the terms.

A simile uses *as* or *like* to compare two dissimilar things. To illustrate: He's fit as a fiddle or He's like an old sore-tailed bear. Similes are commonly used in dialogue. Western lingo is replete with such sayings, many of them quite humorous. Some are also off-color and uncouth, for Western humor tends to be a bit ribald. A sprinkling of these sayings imparts flavor to any book.

Similes are used just as frequently within the narrative. In first-person narration, a simile has much the same effect as it would in dialogue. The reason, of course, is that the first-person narrator seems to be speaking directly to the reader. In third-person narration, similes must be used with discretion. The author, speaking in an omniscient voice, can credibly relate: The wind was like a cold knife. On the other hand, he cannot relate: It was cold as a well-digger's ass. The reader would never accept such a colloquial sound from an omniscient narrator.

A metaphor is somewhat more complex. Though it makes a comparison, it is less direct than a simile. The reader must make the connection for himself, and thereby draw a mental image. To illustrate: He'd cut off his nose to spite his face. Such metaphors are commonly used in dialogue. Westerners pepper their speech with these sayings, some humorous and some downright vulgar. Many are so familiar that they have the ring of a cliché. The trick for the writer is to create something original. A new image.

Metaphors are equally useful within the narrative. Here again, the distinction between first person and third person must be taken into account. Either one, in speaking about a character, might relate: He was on the sundown side of forty. However, the third-person narrator would never relate: She squawked worse than a broken-billed duck. Virtually anything can be used to construct a metaphor, from animals to the weather. All it requires is two dissimilar objects and a twist to give it originality. Words entwined to produce images.

The experienced writer uses simile and metaphor with restraint. In my third published novel, I pulled out all stops. Every character had his own repertoire of simile and metaphor. Not to be outdone, the third-person narrator (that's me) scattered them at random throughout the narrative. After reading the manuscript, the editor gave me a call. Somewhat amused, he said: "Wouldn't you like to save a few metaphors for your next book?" We compromised and he performed editorial surgery with his red pencil. The novel benefited greatly in the process.

The writer benefited as well. Upon reading the copyedited manuscript, I gained further insight into my craft. Simile and metaphor are important elements in the development of a writer's style. To a large degree, they personalize his style, add something unique to his voice. Yet the experience taught me that simile and metaphor can be used to excess. Too much, no matter how well done, distracts the reader and intrudes on the story. The lesson, like so many lessons having to do with writing, can be reduced to a truism. All good things in moderation.

Scene by Scene

A favorite device of many writers is to open the book with action in progress. If it's done well, the reader will immediately be caught up in the story. I opened *The Manhunter* with an actual bank robbery by Jesse James and his boys. The opening scene of *The Kincaids* was an accurate portrayal of how a hide hunter blasts his way through a buffalo herd. The action in progress could even be something ordinary, such as a roundup or a broncbuster at work. The trick is to render it with excitement and detailed realism. Your goal is to get the reader's attention, surprise him with an action sequence at the very outset. Whether narrative, or narrative mixed with dialogue, show something happening that will get the reader involved. Hook him with action.

Later in the chapter you can provide the background material relevant to the opening scene. Or, in many instances, you'll find it works equally well to delay presenting background material until the second chapter. In *The Big Sky*, A. B. Guthrie opened with a fistfight between Boone Caudill, the protagonist, and his father. Only later, in the second chapter, does the reader begin to understand Boone and the setting of the story. The first chapter is all motion and conflict, characters in action. The reader is instantly involved, and so intrigued by the father and son brawl that he wants to learn more. Guthrie got things off to a fast start and he made the reader care what happens to these people. That's Western writing at its best.

A scene might be defined as an unbroken flow of action. There's no time lapse or jumping about from one setting to another. To be vivid and suspenseful, the scene should be *enacted* by the characters. Long passages of narrative and exposition tend to slow the pace and distract the reader. Events might pause briefly for some needed background explanation or a moment of inner monologue. But when the action resumes, the characters should play out the scene without major interruption to its end. Whether an action sequence or action mixed with dialogue, the scene must somehow advance the story line. Then, by the smoothest transition possible, the story progresses to the next scene. Novels are written in just that manner, scene by scene by scene. Every scene informs the reader and provides revelation of character and actionizes events. All the scenes are interlocked and ultimately join to form the whole. The novel.

Action, Conflict, and Suspense

Action is a mainstay of the Western novel. But gratuitous action, one action scene after another, makes for dull reading. Nor must action sequences involve the obligatory fistfight or gunfight. Man against nature—a blizzard or a prairie fire—can be as harrowing as man against man. Pace the action so that it dovetails realistically with the story line.

How do you achieve pace in a novel? What creates the momentum that propels a reader onward in the story? Unfolding events lead naturally to other events, and a periodic crisis. Action, conflict, and suspense blend to establish pace.

There are many literary devices for creating suspense. A character subjected to a physical hazard is the most apparent. The threat can also be emotional, a looming crisis in a personal relationship. Or the threat of economic ruin, whether by the forces of nature or at the hands of an adversary. Surprise itself can place a character in jeopardy. The unexpected, whether in the form of an ambush or a cattle stampede, raises the specter of danger. A challenge of any sort, from a poker game to a gunfight, lends an atmosphere of uncertainty. Any act that raises the possibility of grave ramifications serves to heighten suspense.

Another indispensable tool for creating suspense is the cliffhanger. By definition, it arouses anxiety in the reader by leaving a character teetering on the brink of disaster. Used at the end of a scene, or the end of a chapter, the cliffhanger freezes everything in midaction. Traditionally a physical action, it most commonly leaves the character suspended in a life-threatening situation. However, an emotional cliffhanger can be equally effective in producing an aura of suspense. A sympathetic character, left in an emotional lurch, often proves quite compelling. Of course, the reader knows the dilemma will ultimately be resolved. What he doesn't know is how or when it will be brought to resolution. That sharpened anticipation keeps him turning pages.

To be effective, a cliffhanger must be an integral part of the plot. Otherwise the reader will realize he's being manipulated by the writer. When a cliffhanger ends a chapter, it can be followed by an immediate continuation of the scene in the next chapter. The most effective cliffhanger, however, is one followed by a complete shift of scene. The writer then builds implicit belief that the characters in the new scene will eventually be brought together with the character left hanging. In this fashion, the suspense is prolonged by presenting a parallel story that promises to resolve the cliffhanger. Done well, it hooks even the most sophisticated reader.

Good writing satisfies the reader's logic, but it also plays on the reader's emotions. Anticipation generates suspense. There must be momentary doubt about the outcome of every scene, and a larger doubt regarding the outcome of the book. When those doubts exist, the reader will identify with the characters. He will be concerned with their ultimate fate, inevitably caught up in their struggle to prevail.

The opening scene will often lay the groundwork for suspense throughout the balance of the book. That first emotional response sometimes determines the reader's involvement for the entire story. A great many writers believe the opening line should startle the reader. In effect, it serves as a hook to grab the reader's attention. Whether it deals with action, mood, or a character, the opening line, even the opening paragraph, can be used to engage the reader. After the initial hook, perhaps it will take several pages, or the whole of the first chapter to establish the tone of the book. That's perfectly acceptable, so long as the hook works. Your reader will stick around to see what happens.

The End

The closing scene in a novel requires equally careful consideration. You must work out a resolution that is at once convincing and conclusive.

Don't leave loose ends until the last page and then try to tie it all together with a lengthy summation. Instead, clear up subplots and any dangling threads sometime before the climactic moment. Otherwise you run the risk of writing your characters into an anticlimax. That is to say, a very dull ending.

In a typical Western plot, the climax comes about when the protagonist and the antagonist confront one another for the last time. The scene demands a resolution all its own, and a touch of inventiveness. The traditional climax has the hero downing the villain in a High Noon gunfight. Yet the writer has options that are equally dramatic. Instead of a gun, perhaps the protagonist subdues his adversary with his fists. Or perhaps he resorts to a gun only after being forced into defending his life. Or perhaps, after the villain's capture, the actual climax occurs with a gallows scene. The point is that the resolution has only one mandatory element: the reader must be assured that justice has been done. How justice is served matters far less than the fact that it is served. The writer can present an unconventional ending and still satisfy the reader.

There are times when a book simply won't end with the climactic moment. The writer then faces an uphill task known as the "denouement." In effect, the denouement is a *final* resolution. Perhaps the protagonist's personal life needs to be set in order. There's a romance or family affairs that deserve their own endings. Or perhaps there's a relationship between major characters that demands a final moment. A last page to put the world right.

To write a denouement, your imperative is that you leave the reader emotionally satisfied. The last page of your book should be as powerful as the climactic moment between the protagonist and his adversary. Anything less will cause the reader to feel let down, gypped. Quite often the denouement will require an entire scene, several pages of dialogue and narrative. You must write it with the same forethought and precision that went into the rest of the novel. The closing lines particularly merit your hard scrutiny.

Perhaps the ending will reflect the theme of your book. Or perhaps the characters will dictate their own ending. They are, after all, the ones who lived the story. Oftentimes the mood of the characters themselves will determine whether you leave the reader feeling happy or sad, thoughtful or euphoric. Notice we're talking here about emotion, what the reader *feels* when he reads those last lines. Your obligation as a writer is to leave him feeling that the story has ended on a satisfactory note. Exactly the way it would have ended had he written it.

Give those last lines every resource at your command. Write an ending that will remain with the reader whenever he thinks of your novel. Pride of craft should allow you to do nothing less.

Three Distinct Voices

Earlier, I remarked that every writer has a distinct voice. The sound of that voice as we read the words represents his style. The cadence, rhythm, and tone of the voice all resound in the ear and create an impression. To illustrate the point, I've selected excerpts from the works of three Western novelists. Let's listen as they speak to us through a third-person narrator. Note the sound of their words.

A. B. Guthrie, in *The Big Sky*, relates a moment in the life of his protagonist, Boone Caudill. The scene takes place at the annual rendezvous of mountain men and traders.

> *Boone rested back on his elbows, feeling large and good, feeling the whiskey warming his belly and spreading out, so that his arms and legs and neck all felt strong and pleasured, as if each had a happy little life of its own. This was the way to live, free and easy, with time all a man's own and none to say no to him.*

Dee Brown, in *Conspiracy of Knaves*, depicts the reaction of a character named Eberhart. The scene takes place during the Civil War, in a Union prison camp.

> *Eberhart was shocked by the appearance of Truscott and the others, their once young faces growing old from boredom and frustration, their skins yellowing from untreated sickness and bad food, their eyes deadening in the demeaning atmosphere. Prisons were the dark side of war, the aging Briton admitted to himself, in some ways worse than death on the field of battle.*

Elmer Kelton, in *The Good Old Boys*, recounts the misgivings of Hewey Calloway. The scene takes place in the barn, with Hewey's nephews, Cotton and Tommy.

Hewey had rather have taken a whipping with a wet rope than face the reception he knew he would get from Eve. It would be colder than a witch's kiss. He put it off as long as he could, taking the horses to the barn, unsaddling, pouring out oats. Cotton came from the house to see his brother and his uncle. Hewey found no cheer in his nephew's face.

Study the three excerpts at length. Note the choice of words, the difference in sentence structure, and the tone of the third-person narrator. Try reading each of them aloud, listening for cadence and rhythm rather than the words themselves. You will hear three distinct voices, each unique unto itself. No one would mistake one for the other, for all three speak to us in a way that imparts a singular impression. That's style.

You may prefer the sound of one writer over the other two. You may have difficulty deciding which sound lingers longer, somehow sticks in your mind. The point here is that you gain insight into style by a detailed examination of how various writers achieve a unique voice. Just as they constructed it, so do you take it apart and subject it to scrutiny. What you like and what you don't like are largely immaterial at the moment. Your first goal is to determine how they do it, what makes each of them sound different. When you've figured that out, you will have cleared a major hurdle. You will comprehend how you might craft your own voice.

Echoes and Sparks

All good writing has about it a certain gusto. Yet we're stumped for an explanation as to what ignites words and summons mental images. There is no infallible guide to style, no inflexible rule by which a writer shapes his own voice. Style is the sound of words on paper, and a unique sound can never be achieved with mannerisms or tricks. Instead, style emerges from simplicity and orderliness. A shorter sentence makes a stronger sentence, and brevity imparts vigor to prose. The concrete is more expressive than the abstract, and particulars reported in detail arouse the imagination. Word pictures evolve from sound, and sound evolves from the way a certain combination of words are ignited. How you strike the spark makes you different from all other writers. The spark itself resounds as your voice.

Osmosis plays a part in every writer's search for style. By nature, most writers are devout readers. Some are omnivorous readers, hop-scotching from genre fiction to mainstream novels to the classics. Whatever your particular reading habits, it cannot help but influence you as a writer. Whether you read A. B. Guthrie or Ernest Hemingway, some of it rubs off. Perhaps you analyze as you read, gathering pointers on technique. Or perhaps it's unconscious, absorbing certain elements with no real awareness. All the while, the process of osmosis is at work. Your writing will ultimately reflect some of what you've read. That's not only normal, it's unavoidable. No writer finds his own voice in a sterile vacuum. His style, in part, will always echo other voices.

There are no shortcuts. Your search for style represents a lifelong jour-ney. What you wrote a year ago will differ from what you write today. So, too, will today's work differ from what you write next year. Some inde-finable change manifests itself with every book you write. With time comes growth and maturity, and constant refinement in style. In a sense, it's similar to a belief common among Indians. Their wise men observed that only the earth and sky endure forever. All else changes.

A writer, if he's lucky, never stops growing.

Cross Cr.
Pompeys
PILLAR
DRY FORK
YELLOW STONE R.
Beauvais Fork
BIGHORN R.
CLARKS PASS
Stillwater
BIG ROSEBUD
ROCKY F.
PRIORS R.
CLARKS F.
HEART MTS.
Stinking R.
Hot Springs
Coullers Mill
Falls
YELLOW STONE LAKE
Volcanic Basin
Ocean Water
No Wood Cr.
Grey Bull R.
No Water Cr.
De Noir
North Fork
Owl Cr.
FREMONTS PEAK & PASS
WIND RIVER RANGE
Wind River
SHELL R.
ABSARAKA
Granite Ridges
St. Mary's
FORT BONNVILLE
NEW FORK
SWEET WATER R.
SOUTH PASS

7.
The Mechanics
of Storytelling

To outline or not to outline? Pardon the pun, but there's the question for the beginning writer. A working outline serves as an invaluable tool for many writers. Others consider it a sort of straightjacket, serving only to immobilize creativity. Still another group looks upon it as a casual reference device, identifying little more than prominent landmarks. Some think it's nothing more than a crutch for the insecure and unimaginative. What really makes the point are all these mixed metaphors dealing with the same subject. Opinion clearly differs with regard to the matter of outlines.

Perhaps a good starting point would be to define what we're talking about here. There are actually two types of outlines, each constructed for a different purpose. (1) A working outline is essentially an expanded synopsis of the story. Plot and characters, sometimes specific scenes, are integrated into the outline. (2) An outline for submission to publishers is essentially a sales presentation. This sort of proposal is usually somewhat abbreviated, a quick-read synopsis.

Spontaneity and Tap Dancers

Let's first consider the diversity of opinion that surrounds a working outline. An argument can be made than an outline serves no useful purpose. Some writers work from a rough mental conception of plot, theme, and character. They shove a piece of paper in the typewriter and take off from wherever they've determined the novel should start. For the most part, there's no formal structure to what they've envisioned in their heads. All options are kept open, and anything can happen along the way. Hence, no need for an outline.

These writers are confident that the story will evolve in the writing.

They have no idea what will happen page to page, let alone chapter to chapter. In fact, they have no real notion of how many chapters the book will eventually require. Nor are they any more certain with regard to characters and characterization. They trust that characters will appear as needed and that character development will occur naturally as the story progresses. Theme, motivation, and plot twists unfold from minute-by-minute improvisation. For them, it all seems somehow inspired.

The operative word here is freedom. These writers view an outline as a form of self-imposed tyranny. They will not be bound by what they perceive as a device that inhibits creativity. Nor will they sacrifice spontaneity for structure, believing the terms to be mutually exclusive. Whatever turn the story takes must occur with a sort of spontaneous combustion, igniting from within. To them, an outline would douse the fires of innovation and originality. Freedom to create means no limitations, no restraints, no predetermined course of events. In short, no outline.

Other writers take a betwixt and between position. They feel there are advantages to an outline, but only if it's short. Anything longer than a page or two seems to them unnecessarily elaborate and overcomplicated. Their principal use of an outline is to develop some sense of story, and the direction it will take. Within the outline, they establish a beginning and an end, and highlight the key events along the way. Their plot has definition, though it still lacks detail. Their characters are in the wings, not yet onstage. While they know the primary roles, they don't know how those roles will be played out. In fact, they don't want to know. The outline stops there.

Here again, the operative word is freedom. Like the advocates of no outline, these writers believe that spontaneity suffers from an abundance of detail. Their outline has the bare bones of the story and they prefer to flesh it out as it's written. Plot and theme will assume substance as events rush forward in natural progression. Their characters will come to life through cause and effect, action and reaction. All those unpredictable twists and turns are viewed as an asset rather than a liability. In large degree, they know where they're headed even though they have no clear idea of how they will get there. Yet they have faith in their ability to tap-dance page by page, scene by scene. They rely on a sort of spur-of-the-moment choreography. Inspiration mixed with fast and fancy footwork.

Lots of Western writers adhere to the no outline or minimal outline school of thought. The novels they write are bought and published, and enjoy a wide readership. Some of what they write, like any other literary endeavor, garners critical acclaim and wins awards. Yet their fixation with spontaneity inevitably increases the difficulty of their task. Unlike some genres, the Western assumes a mantle of authenticity through research. The writer who works with no outline, or at best the bare bones, constantly finds himself at odds with the need for realistic detail. Often he proceeds by fits and starts, halting frequently to thumb through his research and integrate the material into the story. His alternative is to let 'er rip in the writing and then shoehorn the research into the rewrite. Either way, he pays a dear price for what he perceives as spontaneity. Some writers consider it too high by far.

Structure and Spontaneity

Over the years I've gotten to know a great many Western writers. The majority of those I've met look upon a working outline as an indispensable tool. They believe an outline is a natural outgrowth of plotting. For them, the plot treats various aspects of the novel with broad strokes. The outline indicates where and how the fine touches will be added. One of the major reasons these writers rely on an outline has to do with research. They contend that better novels result when the research is integrated into the story as it's being written. Their contention is bolstered by the fact that details derived from research comprise a good part of the fine touches, specifically authenticity and realism. I endorse the argument totally.

Some of these writers construct outlines 4-5 pages in length. Others feel 10-20 pages provide a better overview. A small percentage believe that something more extensive, upwards of 30-40 pages, creates the proper framework. Whatever the length, none of them considers the outline an ironbound commitment. In the writing, they will deviate from the outline whenever it improves the story. They know from experience that spontaneity and structure *are not* mutually exclusive terms. An outline in itself doesn't impose limitations on a writer's creativity and originality. What a writer *believes* imposes such limitations. Anyone who doesn't believe in outlines shouldn't use them. End of argument.

For the believers, an outline may take various forms. Some writers, with the plot in mind, simply draft a chronology of events. This provides a general idea of the story line and determines when and where characters will take certain actions. The specifics of those events are not elaborated in any great detail. Instead, the writer accepts that plot twists and insights into character will occur as he delves deeper into the story. To a degree, he puts his subconscious to work and trusts instinct as much as logic. Later, should an idea prove faulty, it can be corrected in the revision stage. The principal purpose of such an outline has to do with the research material. All research is keyed to the chronology of events, adding further substance to the structure. The writer now has a step-by-step plan for crafting his novel.

Other writers follow a logical approach. They first draft a brief synopsis of the plot, usually a couple of pages in length. From the synopsis, they then determine where logic dictates the separation of major events. These major events establish the division of chapters and a natural progression of the story line. Factored into this chapter breakdown are the characters and their actions within the context of unfolding events. At this point, the writer drafts a short paragraph on each chapter, describing what takes place and who's involved. Plot twists are considered; but no great detail is provided regarding character development and motivation. All that will evolve from the writing itself. Finally, the research material is keyed to the appropriate chapters. The outline now charts a course, chapter by chapter, through the novel.

Another group of writers believe in a somewhat more extensive outline. Since I count myself in their number, perhaps my own approach will illustrate the method involved. Unresolved problems bother me, and I prefer to work them out now rather than later. Here, I'm talking about problems that deal with overall structure, problems that become apparent only within an exhaustive outline. As a result, I usually devote a month to planning a project: two weeks for research and two weeks for drafting the outline. When I'm finished, I have a solid structure that imposes a sense of order on the novel. Not that it doesn't change in the writing; nothing is sacrosanct once my characters start living the story. But the few times I've revamped an outline in the midst of writing was to tighten the plot, shorten the number of chapters. Otherwise, the novel takes its marching orders from the outline.

To begin, I think the plot through. This inevitably results in a large pile of scribbled notes involving theme and character and events. I then draft a synopsis of the plot which runs 4-10 pages in length. What I'm after is a general statement of the story line from beginning to end. The length is unimportant so long as the essence of the plot has been reduced to paper. At this point, I stop and analyze the story line for flaws. Quite often, I spot glaring problems that hadn't surfaced during the plotting stage. Addressing the situation now eliminates a problem that might breed other problems within the outline. A still greater benefit is the elimination of problems that might not surface until the writing itself.

The next step involves a chronological breakout. I dovetail fictional plot events with historical events uncovered in the research. These combined events are then listed in an actual time frame, day and date. The chronological breakout enables me to determine where the natural divisions for each chapter will occur. Once I've established a chapter breakdown, I proceed by structuring the scenes within each chapter. In effect, I'm working out the details of the story as I advance farther into the outline. All the while I'm alert to the possibilities of plot twists, cliffhangers, and character development. Structural problems, of course, are always foremost in my mind.

The work to this point has been done with pencil and legal pad. I erase and rewrite and shift dates as well as events. In the evolution there finally occurs an orderly flow of plot, historical incident, and dramatic moment. At that stage, I shift to the typewriter and start with the opening chapter. What results might be termed a minioutline of each chapter, usually a half page in length. I sketch every scene as briefly as possible, highlighting character and action and elements critical to the advancement of plot. Chapter by chapter, scene by scene, I proceed through the book. When it's finished, the outline provides shape and form to the original concept. The last step is to key the research to scenes within each chapter. I now have a detailed blueprint of how the novel will be constructed.

Not all problems have been ironed out. But over the course of the novel there will be damned few surprises. I'm ready to bring the characters onstage and let them reveal how *they* will play out the story I've concocted. Bear in mind, emotion powers fiction, and all emotion stems directly from characters. There's where spontaneity truly shines, where a writer develops a reputation for innovation and originality. He takes the leash off his characters, records their actions and words and emotional upheavals. The story has structure because the outline has been crafted with precision. The novel has immediacy—a sense of life being lived—because the characters perform their roles with passion. That's what separates a ho-hum potboiler from a crackling good yarn.

The way I outline a novel would suffocate many writers. The way some of them tap-dance from scene to scene would leave me stuck on the opening sentence of page one. All of which proves yet again that there's no one way, no right way. Nor is there a wrong way. A writer experiments until he finds the method that suits him best. The single criterion is that it works for him. An outline has no value apart from enabling a writer to write at top form. For certain writers, no outline delivers equal value. You have to decide for yourself which approach has greater merit. The way you'll reach that decision will be the way almost all writers reached theirs. You'll tap-dance awhile and then you'll labor over an outline awhile. In the end, you'll find we all perform on the same stage. How we get there is simply a matter of personal choice.

Outlines For Editors

So much for a working outline. Let's move now to an outline designed for submission to publishers. As mentioned earlier, this type of outline is a proposal, or sales presentation. Your purpose is to enthrall an editor with the concept and story line in a few pages. Editors have a limited amount of time to consider such projects, and thus you have a limited amount of space in which to cinch the sale. No easy task.

Established authors can sell a novel on the basis of an outline alone. In fact, writers with proven track records seldom begin a book until they have a contract in hand. Their reputation for delivering a marketable product permits them to negotiate everything out front. The outlines they submit to publishers are often skimpy, two or three pages at most. On occasion, there's no outline at all. One novel I wrote was sold by my agent describing the premise to a publisher over the telephone. The deal was clinched in less than ten minutes.

That rarely happens with beginning writers. To be absolutely frank, a newcomer seldom sells a novel simply on the basis of an outline. He's an unknown quantity, and publishers are wary of risking money on a speculative venture. However good the outline sounds, the publisher has no assurance that the writer will deliver a salable manuscript. Sometimes a publisher will gamble on the basis of an outline and three sample chapters. But the concept *and* the style of writing have to display an inordinate degree of talent. Even then, the terms offered by the publisher will be less than generous. A low advance and small royalties, the typical boilerplate contract.

There's a more realistic approach to that first sale. Experience demonstrates that a beginning writer vastly increases his chances by completing the manuscript. At that point, the publisher is no longer dealing with an unknown quantity. The manuscript speaks for itself, tangible proof that the writer has crafted a marketable novel. The first book I sold, *Black Fox*, was bought on the basis of a completed manuscript. The second novel, *Mattie Silks*, was purchased on the strength of a half-completed manuscript. To underscore the point, I have never known a beginning writer who sold a novel on the basis of an outline and three sample chapters. I've heard about it and read about it, but no writer of my acquaintance has ever pulled it off. Those rare instances when it does happen merely foster a myth that frustrates and defeats many fine potential novelists. Improve your odds and save yourself a lot of grief on that first effort. Deliver a completed manuscript.

Which brings us back to the outline. Before reading a manuscript, the editor wants some sense of the story, an insight into plot, theme, and character. *You enhance the odds of selling the manuscript by submitting it with an outline.* So you have every reason to write an outline that captures the essence and the impact of your story. (You must also write a humdinger of a query letter, which is covered in Chapter 10.) Your object is to persuade the editor that the novel presents a plausible and compelling tale, one that will appeal to a wide readership. Failing that in the outline, why should the editor bother to read an entire manuscript? Let's rephrase the question along more personal lines. If you write a pedestrian outline, why would the editor believe you'd do any better with the novel itself? Clearly you have incentive to write a convincing outline.

Of course, you shouldn't get carried away. A proposal of this nature should be presented simply and quickly. What's needed is a broad overview that suggests the thrust of your story. An outline 8-10 pages in length provides sufficient detail for the editor to judge the material. An outline from a beginning writer that runs 30-40 pages in length usually has a negative impact. Editors are busy people, and they're oftentimes defeated by a long, overly complex outline. The typical editor might opt instead to read four or five pages of the manuscript. Those four or five pages better grab the editor's attention and convey the sense of the *entire* story. Otherwise, you've just lost a sale. Your best bet is to write a persuasive outline. Entice the editor into the manuscript.

How do you crystallize a story into a few pages? Perhaps the better way would be to show you how it's done rather than tell you. Sometime in the near future I plan to write a traditional Western novel entitled *Tenbow*. The setting of the novel is an imaginary town located in the Wind River Mountains. The characters are imaginary as well, though the protagonist is patterned on an Old West detective. The plot includes elements of mystery and suspense, and the theme is one of retribution. Here's the outline, reproduced in its entirety. Study it with an analytical eye.

TENBOW
By
MATT BRAUN

April, 1878

An unidentified man carefully stalks a rancher. His stealth is catlike, and he's at great pains to leave no sign of his passing. He stays hidden within a treeline and trails his victim to a high mountain meadow. There he takes a steady position and raises the leaf sight on a Sharps buffalo rifle. He kills the rancher with one shot from a distance of four hundred yards.

Cheyenne, Wyoming Territory

Jack Stillman is a private investigator of considerable renown. A former deputy U.S. marshal, his reputation as a manhunter is unsurpassed. In late April, Carl Richter, a wealthy cattleman, arrives at Stillman's office. Richter proposes to retain the detective and offers a substantial fee. The story he tells is at once chilling and mysterious.

A reign of terror has settled over Tenbow Valley, which is located in the Wind River Mountains. Within the past month three small ranchers and one homesteader have been murdered from ambush. The killer methodically stalks his victims, using a long-range rifle. He never leaves a trail.

Richter believes the murders are part of a sinister plot, engineered by one of two men. The first is Will Sontag, an old cattle baron who once claimed the entire valley as his domain. The second is Frank Devlin, an aggressive land speculator new to the valley. Richter asks the detective to halt the murders, and bring the man responsible to justice. Intrigued, Stillman agrees to undertake the case.

One week later Stillman rides into Tenbow. The town is small but prosperous, the only trade center within the valley. There he poses as Duke Drummond, professional gambler. He opens up shop in a saloon, attracting local high rollers to his table-stakes game. One of the saloon girls, Jennie Blake, falls under his spell and becomes an invaluable source of information. He quickly learns that the major suspects in the case are rivals, and openly antagonistic.

Devlin, the speculator, ostensibly buys land for resale to settlers. His sympathies appear to be with the common people, farmers and small ranchers. Sontag, the cattle baron, attempts to outbid Devlin whenever someone decides to sell out. His goal is clearly to regain control of the valley, which was open grazeland prior to the Homestead Act. Fear pervades the valley, and there's widespread belief that the murders are intended to drive people from their land. Stillman concludes that Sontag is the most likely suspect.

Leaving Tenbow, Stillman assumes yet another disguise. He passes himself off as an itinerant broncbuster and takes a job with Sontag's outfit. Within days, he discovers that Sontag has secretly imported Jud Holt, a hired gun for the infamous International Cattlemen's Association. Sontag's pretext for recruiting the gunman is that nesters and small ranchers are rustling his cattle.

Stillman immediately suspects Holt of committing the murders. His suspicion seems justified when another farmer is killed; the murder occurs on a day when Holt is absent from the ranch. The next time Holt rides out alone, Stillman trails him. It soon becomes evident that Holt is conducting a search of his own, probing deep into the mountain wilderness. Holt follows a meandering course, and there seems no ready explanation for his actions.

Upon returning to the ranch, Stillman learns that the

county judge has been murdered. His attention shifts from Sontag and Holt to Frank Devlin, the land speculator. Judge Vance Taggart had been Devlin's most outspoken opponent.

Stillman returns to Tenbow. Once more posing as a gambler, he manages to strike up an acquaintance with Devlin. He also meets Monty Johnson, a hard case who acts as the speculator's bodyguard. Devlin explains Johnson's presence by saying he pays cash for land, and therefore needs protection. Stillman feels there's a better explanation: Monty Johnson might very well be a hired assassin.

Yet, upon digging further, Stillman uncovers no proof. Devlin and Johnson apparently never leave town except on land deals. None of their trips coincides with the murder dates, and they have an ironclad alibi for the day of Judge Taggart's murder. Stillman nonetheless senses something fishy about Devlin. Subtle interrogation, aided by several drinks, reveals that Devlin's previous headquarters was in Laramie. Stillman decides to play a hunch.

Traveling to Laramie, Stillman undertakes an investigation into Devlin's background. He learns, through law enforcement contacts, that Devlin has been involved in many shady deals. Almost by happenstance, he discovers that the railroad has secret plans to build a spur line to Tenbow. The obvious conclusion is that Devlin somehow learned of the plan, and then set about buying up land in Tenbow Valley. To scare the settlers into selling, it follows that Devlin would have orchestrated the string of murders. By buying cheap, Devlin could wait for the spur line to be built and then reap enormous profits. The premise becomes all the more believable when Stillman returns to Tenbow. In his absence, another small rancher has been murdered.

Stillman quietly investigates the murder. Once again, however, he's unable to establish any direct link to Devlin. He determines to take matters into his own hands; it seems the only way to stop the killings. That evening, he braces Devlin in the land company office. A furious brawl ensues between Stillman and Monty Johnson. Afterward, with Johnson out cold, Stillman subjects Devlin to a rough grilling. The land speculator admits everything regarding his scheme to profit from the spur line. But he adamantly denies any knowledge of the murders, and sticks to his story. Halfway convinced,

Stillman finally leaves and walks to the saloon. There he learns that the killer has struck again. Samuel Packard, the county prosecutor, has just been murdered.

Overnight, Stillman concludes there is some hidden motive behind the murders. He's now convinced that neither Devlin nor Sontag is involved. He pays a call on the sheriff, revealing both his identity and the results of his investigation. He's looking for anything that will establish a connection among the victims.

In questioning the sheriff, Stillman stumbles upon a common denominator. Several years ago, a man by the name of Joe Quinn had been brought to trial on a charge of attempted rape. A former mountain man, Quinn at the time was working as a wolf trapper for Will Sontag. The woman he had allegedly attempted to rape was Sontag's wife. Some doubt existed as to Quinn's guilt, but he'd nonetheless been convicted and sentenced to prison. Judge Taggart had tried the case; Samuel Packard had been the prosecutor; and the other murder victims had sat as members of the jury. The sheriff ends his recounting with the most telling comment of all. Scarcely two months past, he'd received notice that Joe Quinn had been paroled. Which was approximately one week before the killings began.

Stillman arrives at Sontag's ranch too late. The cattleman is dead, cut down by a single rifle shot. However, due to a light rain during the night, the killer has at last left a trail. Stillman tracks Quinn through the mountains for two days. He finds spots where Quinn stopped and watched him from a distance; it slowly becomes apparent that Quinn does not want to kill him. Yet Stillman is relentless in his pursuit, and alert now for an ambush. Quinn resorts to evasive tricks known only to Indians and mountain men; Stillman's woodslore enables him to keep pace. Both men are living off the land, eating berries and snaring small game. Finally, on the third day, Quinn lays an ambush. He wounds Stillman and leaves him for dead.

Stillman binds his wound and resumes the chase. The trail is easier to follow, for Quinn no longer believes he's being pursued. On the fourth day, Stillman surprises him at dawn, in a remote campsite. When Quinn tries for his horse, Stillman fires a warning shot. Quinn takes to the woods on foot, and Stillman follows. Gradually, Stillman becomes aware that Quinn is using a favorite tactic of grizzly bears: he's circling back in an effort to jump the hunter from the rear. Quietly, like predators, they stalk each other in the dense woods and rocky terrain. Stillman finally outwits him and springs a trap. Quinn refuses to surrender, and opens fire. Stillman reluctantly kills him.

Upon returning to Tenbow, Stillman reports to Carl Richter. He learns that Devlin, fearing exposure, has departed town. Sontag's wife, moreover, has confessed to falsely accusing Quinn of attempted rape. He was, instead, her secret lover; she'd made the charge only after her husband had become suspicious. Quinn's retribution would have ultimately claimed the lives of all involved. With the case closed, Stillman prepares to leave.

Then, unexpectedly, he is confronted on the street by Jud Holt. The International's gunman accuses him of withholding information—playing a lone hand—and thereby causing Sontag's death. Stillman attempts to reason with him, but to no avail. Holt needs a scapegoat to absolve himself with the International for Sontag's death; Stillman is the obvious candidate. In the end, Holt forces a showdown and Stillman kills him. It seems to Stillman a senseless death.

Jennie Blake has no such qualms. She revels instead in the fact that Stillman has emerged alive from the ordeal. That evening, in her room over the saloon, they hold a private celebration all their own. Yet there is a bittersweet quality about their last night together. Jennie knows she will never see him again.

Late the next morning Stillman rides out of Tenbow. He's grown attached to Jennie, but there is no thought of taking her along. His way of life permits few personal ties and nothing of a permanent nature. High atop a distant mountain pass, he pauses for a final look at the valley. What sticks in his mind is perhaps the oddest aspect of the case.

For all their differences, Joe Quinn and Jud Holt were very much alike. Stillman considers it ironic but nonetheless true.

Some men live out their lives waiting to be killed.

The outline for *Tenbow* accomplishes several things. There's a strong sense of the story line and the underlying theme. The characters are identified by their roles rather than sketched in detail. Yet they appear interesting and plausible, capable of intriguing the reader when fully drawn. The plot promises twists and turns, with a balanced mix of action, conflict, and suspense. There's an element of mystery that sets it apart from commonplace traditional Westerns. Finally, with a touch of irony, the resolution indicates that justice has been served. In short, a genre Western with a difference.

The *Tenbow* outline wasn't written to astound or amaze. It's a workmanlike job which highlights all the elements critical to a good novel. Nothing spectacular, certainly no candidate for the Pulitzer Prize. But it's the kind of Western that will enjoy wide readership and make money for the publisher. You might consider reading it a second or a third time, analyzing how it was structured to work as a sales presentation. For in the end, that's the single goal of such a proposal. To entice an editor through the medium of an outline.

It's how writers get contracts for their books.

Over the years I've talked with many fledgling writers. I've chaired panels at seminars, lectured at universities, and met one-on-one with dozens of struggling craftsmen. A central question in all these discussions has to do with the working outline. There's a good deal of ambivalence about it, and quite often considerable resistance. In my experience, all too many beginning writers have an image of themselves as an artist. From that stems the misconception that an outline stifles creativity. It is my personal belief that this misconception works to the detriment of the aspiring writer. While it's not the sole reason, it's one of the major reasons so many of them remain an "unpublished author." Only a small percentage of successful writers tap-dance their way through a novel. The rest of us labor to create a blueprint of what we will write before we write it. Perhaps that's the difference between artists and craftsmen.

Yet there's more to it than the matter of outlines. We're talking about differing views on the profession of writing. Intellectuals versus wordsmiths, and widely diverging opinions on how a novel gets written. Whatever middle ground exists generally becomes lost in the argument.

As a result, the critical issue rarely benefits from open discussion. No one addresses the underlying cause of the differences. Nor do they identify it by name.

So we'll discuss it in the next chapter. We'll put it into perspective and identify it by name. A subject all unto itself.

We're talking discipline.

CHEYENNE RIVER
PINE CR.
CLEAR WATER
BEAR BUTTE
Bear Cr.
BOX ELDER
BLACK HILLS
HARNEYS PEAK
SPRING C
RAPID
ELK
MAUVAIS TERRE
Corn Cr.
Eagle Nest
Porcupine Cr.
Porcupine Tail
Wounded Knee
White Earth
HAT CR.
SAGO CR.
OLD WOMANS FK.
Bad Hand
Earth Lodge
Antelope
Rush Cr.
Dancers Hill
NIOBR
FT LARAMIE
CHIMNEY ROCK
COURTHOUSE ROCK
FT MITCHELL
Cold Water
Blue Water
SCOTTS BLUFF
PUMPKIN CR.
ASH CR.
GRATTAN
Julesburg
FT SEDGWICK
DEVILS SMOKE HOUSE
To Denver
SOUTH PLATTE
Crow Cr.
BLUFFS
Antelope

8.
Inspiration vs.
Perspiration

A writer punches no time clock. He's effectively his own boss and therefore answerable to no one but himself. Whether he works today, or decides to play hooky, will be determined on the basis of self-discipline. For nothing describes the writing process quite so aptly as the word *discipline*. Innovation and creativity are necessary to doing it well. Discipline gets it done.

Writers are a diverse lot. I know some who can't write unless they're facing an imminent deadline. I know others who invent excuses to put off until tomorrow what should have been done today. Conversely, I know several compulsives, writers who can't let a day pass without a stint at the typewriter. However, the majority of my writer acquaintances are neither compulsives nor slackards. They discipline themselves instead to a daily routine.

A certain group of writers prefer the morning hours. They feel their most productive time is immediately following a night's sleep. Another group believes the afternoon hours are the most productive. Their mornings are reserved for errands or reading or whatever strikes their fancy at the moment. All these writers, whether they work mornings or afternoons, have one thing in common. Their workday lasts roughly four hours. Never much more. Never much less. Four hours does it.

These writers subscribe to the hoariest myth of the profession. There is a belief, perpetuated through the generations, that a writer can be creative only *four hours* a day. All but holy writ, the belief has gained widespread acceptance within the literary community. Of course, what it actually represents is the world's best excuse not to work a full day. After four hours at the typewriter, the creative juices automatically go dry. The balance of the day can then be devoted to all manner of pleasurable activities.

Nothing could be more at odds with reality. A legion of writers past and present belie the myth. Some of them work all day, six or seven days a week, writing straight through until the novel is completed. Others work a normal eight-hour workday, five days a week, with a break on the weekend. Their creative juices continue to flow because they impose no limitations on themselves. By contrast, the four-hours-a-day group simply stops on the stroke of the clock. Life's a helluva lot more fun that way.

Still another group works on a quota system. Let's suppose a writer sets a daily production quota of five pages. Whether he starts in the morning or the afternoon is largely immaterial. He forces himself to sit there until he's knocked out the requisite number of pages. On a good day, he might hit the mark in three or four hours. On a rough day, he might labor for ten hours or more. Time doesn't matter; the quota's the thing. In the end, these writers probably average a workweek fairly close to the forty-hours-a-week-crowd. They differ only on the approach.

What they have in common is discipline. One works straight through until the novel is completed. Another works a conventional forty-hour week. The third works until the daily quota has been produced. All three methods are a form of discipline, establishing routine and schedule. These writers write every day, and they're not concerned with creative juices. Nor do they rationalize or invent excuses for a day away from the typewriter. Their job is to craft novels, and each disciplines himself in his own way until the job's done. That discipline evolves from a universal truth about the profession. Writing is 10 percent inspiration and 90 percent perspiration.

Angst and Antidotes

Yet there are those who worship at the throne of inspiration. They usually write in fits and starts, suffering some form of angst every word of the way. There may be days that begin and end with a blank sheet of paper. There may be days when twenty pages zip through the typewriter. Then there are days, sometimes weeks, when lightning fails to strike altogether. The effect, curiously enough, seldom touches those who advocate creativity through perspiration. Instead, it manifests itself in those who venerate inspiration. It's commonly called writer's block.

By any definition, writer's block results in mental paralysis. One cause might be that the writer doesn't believe in outlining a novel. Winging it scene by scene, he suddenly finds himself at a loss for what happens next. Another cause might be a form of lassitude, wherein the subconscious wills the conscious to take a holiday. Whatever the case, there is an antidote that has performed wonders for many writers. You plant your butt in a chair and discipline yourself to sit there for ten straight hours. Perhaps you won't write a word that day, or the next. But very quickly you'll experience few ten-hour days, and even fewer word-less days. Frustration, not to mention boredom, impacts mental attitude. One such day usually suffices to cure the paralysis of writer's block. Discipline, in short order, acts as an elixir.

No doubt you've heard a good deal of discussion about writer's block. At seminars and symposiums, even in creative writing courses, the subject is presented as a matter of grave consequence. Writer's block, we're led to believe, happens to every novelist at some point in his career. Some writers, we're told, experience it on a regular basis, like migraine headaches. Others, to use a baseball analogy, undergo cyclical slumps, like a star player whose batting average mysteriously drops off. The conventional wisdom has it that you must somehow ride out these periods of creative paralysis. Take a few days off and then start fresh. Work on another project for a time, and come back to the troublesome novel with a new perspective. Consult with another writer whose objective viewpoint will guide you through the impasse. Or, in extreme cases, go see a psychiatrist. Lots of famous authors depend on a shrink to unblock their heads.

To the conventional wisdom, I say balderdash! Not that I dispute the existence of writer's block. I've known several writers who experienced this strange, recurrent malady. In every instance, however, these were writers who considered themselves "artists." Their work was literature with a capital L, some high art form that fed on intellect and inspiration. On the other hand, I have never known a professional storyteller who suffered creative paralysis. These are the craftsmen and wordsmiths of our trade, the working pros who have neither the time nor the tolerance for writer's block. They look upon the literati as pompous elitists, who occasionally produce a novel with widespread appeal. Their job involves weaving tales and entertaining the public, crafting genre novels with precision. They write without pretense or artifice. They simply do their job.

One Writer's Viewpoint

All of this was unknown to me when I began writing. As mentioned earlier, I holed up in a mountain cabin and took a year to find out whether I had the talent to write Western novels. I was ignorant of the four-hour creative myth and writer's block and the need for artistic inspiration. I thought the inspired part took place when a writer plotted and outlined his story. Thereafter, in my mind, he sat down at the typewriter and went to work. To me, writing was like any other job, albeit one of enormous personal satisfaction. I figured you started a book, worked like hell to capture images on paper, and kept at it until the manuscript was completed. I set a chapter a day as my goal.

The chapters in those early books were 8-10 pages in length. Later, I experimented with chapters some twenty pages in length, broken down into five or six scenes. But in the beginning, I was shooting for roughly ten pages a day. I began work at nine o'clock in the morning and stayed with it until the chapter was finished. Sometimes I wrapped it up by four or five o'clock in the afternoon. Oftentimes, after a break for supper, I worked until nine or ten at night. There were many days when I sat at the typewriter a total of twelve hours. I simply wasn't aware that my creative juices had stopped eight hours previously. I kept on working at full speed.

Of course, as it happened, speed wasn't my forte. I discovered that I was a slow, thoughtful writer. Every sentence was constructed and reconstructed many times before I put it down on paper. I often toyed with a sentence fifteen minutes or more, waiting until it sounded right in my head. I assumed the whole idea of writing was to get it the way you wanted it the first time out. That meant long hours at the typewriter, and lots of time spent staring off into space. But when I finally typed a sentence, it was as good as I was capable of writing at that particular moment. I was too stubborn to compromise and too intent on getting it right. I sweated every sentence.

A routine soon developed. I worked six days a week, averaging eight hours a day. Every morning, over a final cup of coffee, I proofread what I had written the day before. I never rewrote it, even though I might change a few words here and there. Instead, the proofreading got me into the thrust of the story and mentally conditioned me for the day's work. I followed this routine for the next five years, through 1974. In that time, I wrote ten novels, one nonfiction work, and one screenplay. The first three novels were on-the-job training and never published. The screenplay was equally flawed and has never been optioned. The latter seven novels and the one nonfiction work were published. During that time, I took only three holidays a year: Thanksgiving, Christmas, and New Year's. I hungered to write and I was a hungry writer. Every book completed represented a welcome payday.

Things began to change in 1975. The advances on each book grew larger and the royalties were producing a steady income. Several of the novels were optioned for theatrical movies and television miniseries. While none of them was ever produced, the option money provided an unexpected windfall. It was during this period that I revamped my work routine. I cut the workweek to five days, allowing myself the leisure of a full weekend. The workday was also revised, nine in the morning to six in the evening. Whole hog or nothing, I also permitted myself to start taking vacations. From one week a year, it's now grown to three weeks a year. Of course, all that is predicated on the career goal I've set for myself. I *must* write two books a year. Otherwise, no vacation.

In large part, the obsession to write has been tempered with experience. I've learned that I can stop in the middle of a scene today and finish it off as well or better come tomorrow. When six o'clock rolls around, I quit work and pack it in for the night. I even attempt to escape my characters for the night, creating diversions by shooting pool and reading and watching sports programs on the cable channels. Along the way, I've also discovered that the sedentary life of a writer requires a certain discipline. On the weekends, I split firewood, ride horses, and burn considerable powder on the firing range. Every morning, after breakfast, I perform calisthenics and work out on a boxer's speed bag. Twenty minutes gets the blood pumping and the adrenaline flowing and the cobwebs brushed away. I'm ready to fight the good fight when I head for the office.

Here's a typical workday. It seldom varies by ten minutes on either end. At nine o'clock, immediately following the morning's exercise, I start work. I write straight through for three hours and then take thirty minutes for lunch. By twelve-thirty I'm back at my desk and I write until two, when I take a fifteen-minute coffee break. Somewhere around four, after another two hours of plugging away, I take a second coffee break. Then I resume writing and stay with it until six o'clock. The noontime break and the two coffee breaks allow me to stretch my legs and relax a bit. By the day's end, however, I've put in a solid eight hours. The same schedule holds whenever I'm doing research. I limit my phone calls and I have little tolerance for interruptions. To get the job done, I need forty hours a week.

The day's production varies from five to seven pages. So I average about 1,800 words a day for the week. That's 9,000 words a week, and the Westerns I write usually top 100,000 words. Allowing for the unforeseen, I can generally complete the first draft in something more than three months. Of course, as I'll explain later, my first draft differs only slightly from the final draft. Still, I do rewrite, and that, along with a professional typing job on the manuscript, adds another month. Tack on a month for the original plotting and research and that brings the total to somewhere over five months. Eight hours a day, forty hours a week, equals two novels a year. I've found that it works for me, and thus far I have been able to maintain a steady output. In sixteen years, 1972-1988, I've had published thirty-one novels and three nonfiction works.

During the same period, I also wrote the "bible" for a miniseries and a theatrical screenplay. In TV-land, the bible is a detailed synopsis of the story, often running thirty pages or more. These projects were both commissioned by West Coast producers, and in each instance, I was flown to Hollywood and received the red-carpet treatment. Since the projects were based on novels I'd written, I got option money as well as an extremely handsome fee for the screenwriting. For a variety of reasons, neither the miniseries nor the screenplay was ever produced. The experience was nonetheless enlightening with regard to the strange and wacky world of filmdom. But that's another story, perhaps a book in itself. Tinseltown exceeds its own reputation!

What's the point of this biographical sketch? I've tried to illustrate one approach to the discipline of writing. The method you adopt, whether the quota system or a certain number of hours per day, will be determined by personal choice. Discipline will ensure that you work consistently, within a structured routine. Discipline will generate that steady, day-by-day production that results in books. Discipline will determine how prolific you are throughout the course of your career.

I strongly urge you to avoid the influence of those who depend on intellect and inspiration for their creativity. Inspired intellectuals are seldom prolific, and I've yet to meet one who wrote a Western. On the other hand, I know many craftsmen who regularly produce Western novels of great excellence. *Writing is a discipline and discipline makes the writer.* Keep the axiom in mind when you start the first draft of your novel. You'll never get better advice.

Hardcover vs. Paperback

Let's consider the matter of career orientation. You may think it a non sequitur, far removed from a discussion of discipline. Yet the subject bears directly on any discourse involving literature and commercial writing. You will be known by *what* you write and *how* it's published. Those two factors often determine whether the quality of your work will be recognized. However regrettable, there's a strong measure of elitism in the world of publishing. Nowhere does the prejudice manifest itself more openly than in genre Westerns.

There are essentially three kinds of Western writers. Comprising the first group are hacks who write faster than the speed of light. They churn out formulaic potboilers, the horse operas and shoot-'em-ups. For the most part, their style of writing takes its form from the old penny-a-word pulps. Their novels lack plot or theme, and their comic strip characters spout clichés disguised as dialogue. What they write might best be summarized by Max Brand's oft-quoted remark that "There has to be a woman, but not much of a one. A good horse is much more important." In short, the Western at its worst.

The second group is composed of journeymen storytellers. Their prose may lack polish, but they nonetheless relate a helluva tale. Though the stories oftentimes play off of formula, plot and theme are evident in the structure. The characters are credible, if not wholly rounded, and the dialogue seldom rings a false note. The narrative performs a serviceable job, advancing the story line at a measured pace. There's lots of action, a decent amount of conflict, and an occasional moment of suspense. The obligatory gunfights, not to mention knock-down-drag-out slugfests, are rendered with a fair degree of realism. Authenticity and historical accuracy are not the principal concerns of these journeymen storytellers. Their goal is to present an escapist yarn that harks back to the day when men were men and women were damned glad of it. They do it with a certain flair.

The third group represents the best of the breed. They are master

123

craftsmen, novelists in every sense of the word. Their stories are structured around human conflict and emotion, played out against a backdrop that evokes time and place. Their characters are fully realized, and compelling relationships develop within the framework of the plot. They deal in theme and symbolism and imagery, all interwoven throughout the broader concept. What they write has about it the historical detail and authentic flavor that draws the reader into a world come alive. Were they so inclined, they could write historical novels of any era, any setting. They choose instead to write of the West, depicting a land and a people unique to the American frontier. Their novels recreate an aspect of our national heritage.

What do these three groups of writers have in common? Foremost is the fact that their works are published in original paperback. There are a few exceptions within the third group, writers whose novels are initially published in hardcover. Yet their numbers are quite small, for reasons we'll come to in a moment. For now, the critical point to remember is that publication in original paperback carries with it a long-standing stigma. The literary community, as well as publishers and book reviewers, foster the belief that an original paperback novel cannot have literary merit. Their prejudice toward commercial writing, and Westerns in particular, further stigmatizes such novels. Moreover, where Westerns are concerned, there's rarely any distinction drawn between the hacks and the skilled novelists. Everyone who publishes in original paperback is tarred with the same brush.

That being the case, you may well ask why any writer would *choose* to publish in paperback. We now enter the realm of economics within the publishing world. Let me use my own experience as an illustration. In 1980, I'd had fifteen novels published, three of which were initially published in hardcover. The hardcover novels were broadly reviewed, and all three were sold for paperback reprint. By contract, however, there was a 50-50 split between me and the hardcover publisher on the advance *and* future royalties from the paperback house. That's the norm for the industry, even though the income derived from the paperback usually exceeds what the writer earns from the hardcover edition. In other words, I lost money for the distinction of being published in hardcover. Since then, all of my Westerns have been published as original paperbacks.

Some Western writers opt for the hardcover route. They want recognition from the book reviewers as well as the literary community. Their belief is that literary recognition will ultimately have a spillover effect when the novels are reprinted in paperback. Their hope is that paperback royalties will one day increase to the point that it offsets the 50-50 split with the hardcover publisher. For a small number of such writers, the plan has worked to their benefit. The others continue to pay the price for being published in hardcover. The majority of Western writers by far opt for original paperback. Simple economics dictate that they will make more money over the course of their careers. They also believe that literary recognition for the Western writer seldom translates into dollars. In fact, writers who look upon their work as literature are at some pains to distance themselves from the Western genre. They are frequently heard to remark that they write novels of the West, not Westerns. By the rules of the game, that makes them artists rather than craftsmen.

Original paperback does have its downside. The prevailing view states that it isn't literature unless it's published in hardcover. This snobbish bias has a direct impact where literary awards are concerned. Seldom does a paperback original win an award for literary achievement. So seldom, in fact, that the criterion seems to be hardcover publication rather than the quality of writing. Anyone familiar with the Western field can cite paperbacks of great excellence that have lost to mediocre novels packaged in hardcover. Elitism does exist, and it extends to every corner of the publishing world. Whether it began with academics or book reviewers, or the literary community as a whole, remains a moot point. A paperback original, however finely crafted, will be labeled a Western. The same book, published in hardcover, would be called a novel of the West. End of argument.

All these variables will affect your career orientation. Perhaps you want to write literature in the grand sense of the word. In that case, start with hardcover and stay with hardcover. Of course, some writers begin with paperback originals and work their way up to hardcover. That was the path I followed, only to reverse it for economic reasons. In the Western field, commercial writing inevitably leads to paperback originals. However, should you opt to stick with paperbacks, don't expect to cover your walls with literary awards. There are exceptions, those one-in-a-hundred virtuosos who can straddle the line between commercial writing and literature. Generally, they finance their hardcover novels (which are rarely reprinted in paperback) by writing paperback originals. Somewhere along the way you may discover that you're just such a virtuoso. Your only limitations are those you impose upon yourself.

For now, I suggest you take a hard look at the realities of publishing. Orient your career toward some long-range goal. Whether it's literature or commercial writing boils down to a matter of personal choice. In the end, you'll find that there's only one imperative. You must be content with who you are as a writer. Nothing else matters.

A bestseller author was once asked, "What would you do if the doctor gave you only six months to live?" He replied: "I'd type faster." His response says it all.

Writers live to write. The rest is icing on the cake.

Titles Are Forever

Let's turn now to another matter that bears directly on your career. Writers agonize over titles. In a very real sense, it's like naming a child. Conception, gestation, and delivery sometimes take longer than actual childbirth. So any old name won't do, not for your baby! It has to resound with originality.

The analogy has merit. Your novel will be known by its title. Editors and reviewers, the reading public and your professional peers will remember what's emblazoned on the cover. They may forget character names and a good deal of the story line. But the title will forever be associated with *your* name. You owe it to yourself to make it a corker!

Apart from personal pride, there's an important business consideration. Your novel will share rack space with dozens of Westerns found in bookstores at any given moment. The shelf life of the average Western is roughly one month. If it hasn't sold by then, the wholesaler will strip the cover and return it to the publisher for credit. Your royalty on returns is zero. Not a red cent.

In effect, your book is competing with all those other Westerns on the racks. The title you select carries the enormous burden of attracting the reader, enticing him to pick up *your* Western. Title and cover art, particularly for the unknown writer, are what sells the book. You have a minute or less to sell the potential reader while he's staring at all those titles. You have only one month to sell thousands of copies of your book across the country. You therefore have incentive to select a crackerjack title.

With some Western writers, their reputation alone sells the book. However, that usually takes many years and involves developing a loyal readership. In my own case, it took twelve novels before the publisher displayed my name in larger print than the title. Even then, I still sweated through the process of creating titles that intrigue and attract attention. On my latest novel, number thirty-one, I considered and discarded dozens of titles before making the final selection. Clearly, it gets no easier with time.

Titles also affect editors. Lots of Westerns by lots of unknown writers hit an editor's desk. One with an eye-catching title has an increased chance of being pulled from the pile. The title itself won't cause the editor to fire off a contract. But it may very well cause the editor to read the manuscript with greater interest. Titles are the starting point of any sale, and the most important sale you'll ever make is to that editor. All the more reason to conjure up a lulu.

How do you go about it? In many instances, the theme or subject matter will suggest a title. Perhaps the location of the novel, or something that occurs in the story, will resound in your mind. Titles are often taken from lines in the Bible, not to mention the works of Shakespeare and other notable literary figures. Some writers strive for the unconventional or the unorthodox, the shock effect. Others form unusual word combinations that have nothing whatever to do with the novel. Their intent is to intrigue and grab attention, entice someone to pick up the book. That should be your intention as well.

The quartet of novels I wrote about the Brannock family illustrates several methods. The first title, *The Brannocks*, was designed to set the stage for a generational saga. The second, *Windward West*, was meant to convey a sense of the westward expansion. The third, *Rio Hondo*, was taken from the focal point of the story. The fourth, *A Distant Land*, was fashioned to leave an impression of venturing into the unknown. The point here is that titles evolve from many sources, and only after considerable work. A well-written novel deserves nothing less.

How to Polish Prose

Finally, let's consider the matter of revisions. Wherever writers gather, it's a subject that provokes lively debate. Still, when the debate runs its course, there's one point that draws universal agreement. An axiom of our craft that stands without equivocation. *From brutal editing emerges good writing.*

A bestseller author was once asked, "How do you know when a novel is finished? At what point do you stop rewriting?" He replied, "When the publisher comes and takes it away from me." His response was dead serious, for an idea seldom has the same impact in cold print as it did in the imagination. All writers learn that a chasm separates the origin of a thought and what can be realistically expressed in prose. On paper, in the transition from vision to print, it seems to have lost its magic. To survive as writers, we must come to grips with the fact that nothing we write will ever attain perfection. We must be content with our best effort at a given moment and let it go. Otherwise we would rewrite the same manuscript until hell freezes over. That is to say, forever.

Some writers, upon completing a manuscript, subject it to the critique of other writers. Or submit it to the scrutiny of family, friends, and anyone else who might serve as a sounding board. Then there are the writers who prefer their own counsel, respect no judgment but their own. Secure in that judgment, they complete a project and promptly ship it off to the publisher. No one, including family and friends, gets so much as a glimpse of their work. They await the only verdict that counts, the verdict of an editor.

A third type of writer falls somewhere in between. Apart from my wife, who reads my output on a daily basis, I've never allowed anyone to critique a manuscript. However, in the beginning, I did allow my mentor to critique several books *after* they had been published. In other words, I sought selective counsel, from a writer I genuinely admired. Today, with the exception of my wife and my agent, no one sees a manuscript until it hits the editor's desk. So I do let certain people read it and I weigh their opinions with considerable thought. But beyond that, I trust my gut instinct to tell me what's right and what's wrong. I believe most writers operate in a similar fashion, never wholly objective. Our inner muse tells us when to stop rewriting, and let it go.

Still, no two writers take the same approach to rewriting. Some simply tidy up the first draft and submit it to the publisher. Others believe the rewrite stage is when a book begins to assume its final form. They often write four or five drafts before they're satisfied with the end result. Another group polishes the manuscript page by page, rewriting yesterday's effort before they proceed to the next scene. This day-by-day rewrite appeals to writers who dread the thought of a complete overhaul when the first draft is finished. Doing it in snippets seems somehow less onerous. Yet another group ruthlessly edits and prunes the first draft, performing virtually no rewrite. Clearly, there are endless variations on the theme.

How you approach rewrite depends largely on how you write. A slow, thoughtful writer will rarely go beyond a second draft. All the more so if he lays out a detailed outline in advance. A writer who detests outlines and operates instead on stream of consciousness will often need four or five drafts. A writer who tosses five pages in the wastebasket for every page of finished copy may complete the novel on the first draft. In the final analysis, you must decide how you will write before you'll have any notion of how to rewrite. That usually means a period of trial and error, considerable experimentation. You'll know the best approach when you find it by the simplest of tests. It works.

A personal aside will illustrate the point. The first nine books I wrote were written on a typewriter. As mentioned earlier, I write at a tortoise-like pace, averaging less than a page an hour. Moreover, in those early days, I was still learning my craft. Everything I wrote looked good and sounded good, basically because I didn't know any better. The first draft, as a result, was all but carved in stone. Upon completing it, I edited the typewritten pages with a pencil, changing words here and there, occasionally restructuring a sentence. None of what I did could be termed rewrite, and there was never any thought of a second draft. The editing completed, I gave the manuscript to a typist for a final draft. I then mailed it off to my agent, confident that I'd written a masterpiece. That belief, though unjustified, was aided and abetted by several editors. They accepted what I delivered and vouchered the check. No one asked for revisions.

The turnabout evolved by happenstance. For one thing, my mentor, Jerrold Mundis, taught me to distinguish good writing from bad writing. For another, I finally realized why I finished each day's work with my backbone in knots. Hunched over a typewriter eight hours a day created incredible stress and physical tension. A word processor seemed too akin to a typewriter, so I switched instead to a pencil and a yellow legal pad. Today, I lean back in a cushy chair, completely relaxed, and write with the legal pad balanced across my lap. When I complete the handwritten first draft, I then give it a speedy trip through the typewriter. As I type, I perform a brutal editing job and rewrite anything that needs fixing. What emerges is a polished second draft, the best I'm capable of writing today. I recognize now that it's not a masterpiece, let alone fine literature. But it's a damn good story, well told. The work of a craftsman.

One last word of advice. Don't allow yourself to be too heavily influenced by other writers. Or what you hear in various writing seminars. Or what's taught in creative writing courses. In fact, don't accept what you've read here as holy scripture. Anyone who teaches writing, or writes a book on how to do it, cannot help but voice personal bias. Any writer with a jigger of self-esteem cannot avoid touting his way as the best way. What the hell, it works for him and he's got the publishing credits to prove it. Yet we're all creatures of our own prejudice and we view writing through a prism of subjectivity. I personally think anyone who writes four or five drafts should consult a neurosurgeon. Writers of my acquaintance think I'm nuts for outlining a novel in such meticulous detail. However reasoned, our arguments pro and con change nothing. We still believe what we believe. Hell's bells and little fishes, it works!

So don't accept our words as a sermon from on high. We're all opinionated, and at the same time, we're all still learning our craft. No writer ever fully masters his trade, regardless of his credentials. We can only relate the mechanics of a profession that has no finite answers. None of us really knows what makes the whirligig whirl at optimum speed. You must sift and sort through what we say and adapt it to your own needs. You will find yourself as a writer by writing. You will mature as a writer by experimenting with untried forms. That's the way it works.

No shortcuts. No simplistic solutions. Nothing cut and dried. You get there the way we all got there.

You write the best you can today.

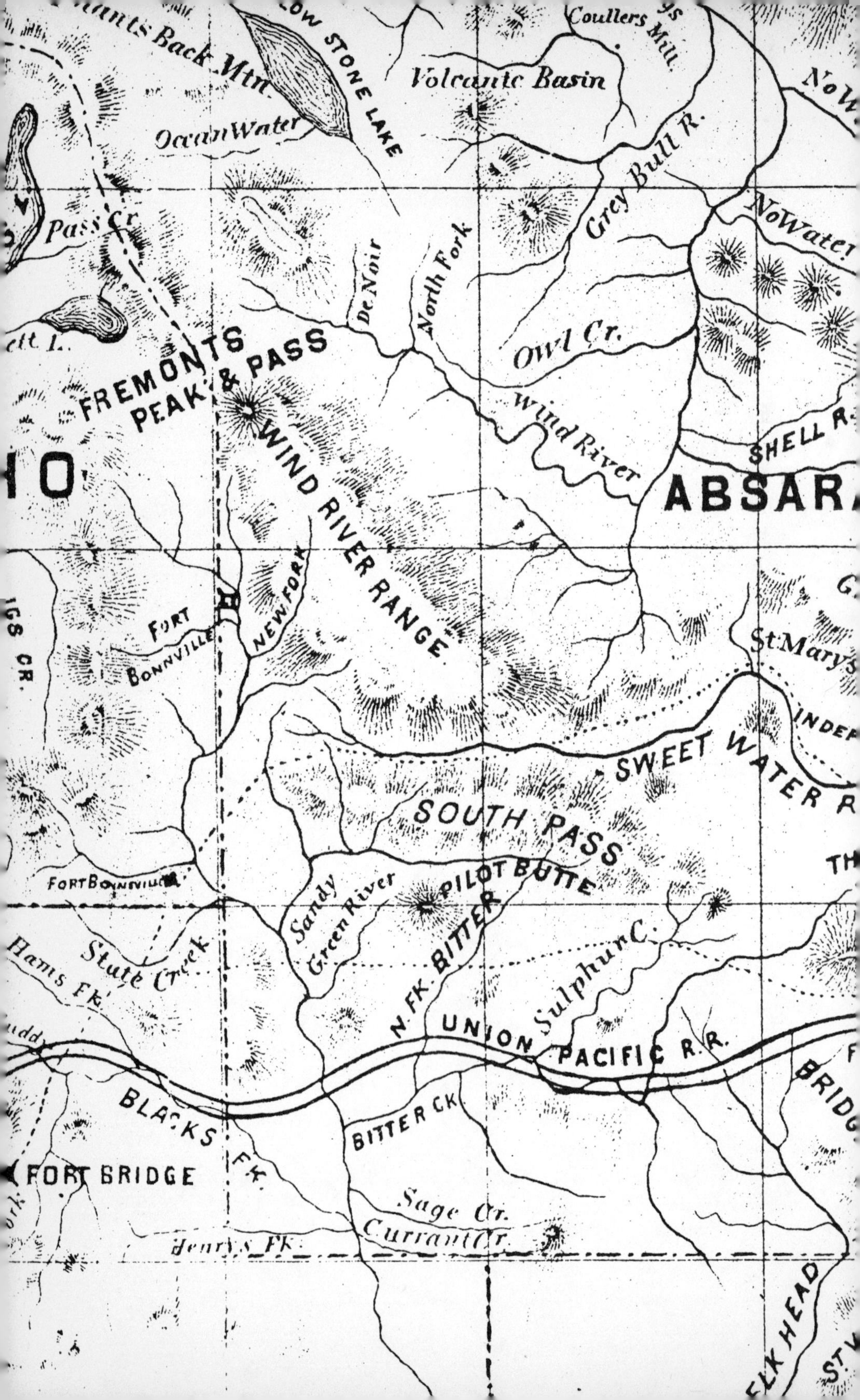

9.
The How and
Where of Research

There is an epic quality to the Western landscape. Those who have traveled it extensively would never question that it is nature's finest work on this continent. Within its timeless spaces are to be found the tallest mountains, the broadest plains, the steepest canyons, and the wildest rivers.

To be authentic, a Western novel must take into account the land. From a historical perspective, the Old West extended from Canada to Mexico, and from the midwestern flatlands to the Pacific Ocean. Found there are barren wastelands and lush valleys, limitless plains and towering mountains, every imaginable type of terrain. Temperatures vary widely, with harsh winters and brutally hot summers prevalent throughout much of the country. In a word, it is a land of paradox. Grandeur and desolation exist everywhere.

From a writer's perspective, the land should be treated as a character within the novel. It was, and remains, a vital force in the lives of Westerners, a force which shapes their day-to-day reality. Because the land looms so large, a writer has an obligation to depict it with the same fidelity that he devotes to other major characters. Westerners have always had a spiritual bond with the land, some spiritual harmony in which the land is a sacred thing as well as a part of the struggle. By any definition, that makes it central to the story.

The background of a Western provides a stage for the characters and a setting for the plot. The skillful writer creates a realistic world for his story, authentic and true to the times. In effect, a milieu reconstructed from archives and historical works. Yet history itself can be used only when it serves the plot, and even then with moderation. Great dollops of history intrude on the story and rarely impress the reader. A novel that seeks to educate rather than entertain has fallen short of the goal.

On-the-Spot Research

The background in your story must withstand close scrutiny. Let's suppose you've decided to use a locale you've never seen. Perhaps it serves as the proper historical setting, or perhaps it simply strikes your fancy. Whichever, you are forewarned against trying to wing it rather than performing the necessary research. Some readers, of course, may never be aware that you've faked it. However, a great many native Westerners will spot it on the instant. And there goes your credibility as a writer.

A personal aside will illustrate the point. In 1985, I began the research on the third and fourth books in the Brannock family saga. Some preliminary digging convinced me that New Mexico Territory in the 1880s was the proper setting. Further, I decided that Santa Fe and the Hondo Valley would represent the focal points. Yet I had never seen the Hondo Valley, had never actually walked it, touched it, and watched a sunset along the waters of the Rio Hondo. I got on a plane and flew to New Mexico.

The first stop was Santa Fe. There, I strolled the ancient plaza and toured the old Governor's Palace. Afterward, I spent an entire day in the state historical library, gathering research material and photocopying faded maps. Among the many things I discovered about the 1880s was that the Anglo government had added its own touch to the area. A bandstand had been erected on the plaza and a white framework facade had been built atop the adobe Governor's Palace. These things have long since disappeared, but they were symbolic of social attitudes that existed during the era. The material provided flavor and substance for the books I planned to write.

The next stop was the town of Roswell. Located in the Pecos Valley, Roswell is but a short drive from the Hondo Valley. I rented a car and spent two days exploring the banks of the Rio Hondo. With an idiot-proof camera, I took a 360-degree series of photos of the valley. Later, the photos were pasted together, creating a panoramic sweep of a valley little changed from the 1880s. While writing the book, the panorama was kept in front of me the entire time. Each day, when I sat down to start work, it was as though I was transported back to that faraway place. The realism, a true sense of the Hondo Valley, showed in the writing.

There is no substitute for physically scouting a location. In 1973, I spent three months traveling by car throughout the West. I clocked 14,000 miles on the odometer and explored the better part of ten states.

At least forty rolls of film were put through the camera, and I collected a small library of research material. At the time, I'd had only three books published, and I could hardly afford such an extensive trip. But my sights were trained on the future, and the investment was returned many times over. From that trip evolved nine novels, each set in a different locale. The authenticity of those novels can be traced to the fact that I was there. I saw it for myself, actually walked it, before I wrote it.

The point by now should be obvious. Whenever possible, go there and experience it for yourself. Take notes on the topography, rivers and streams, the vegetation. Grind away with your camera and record on film the details memory would never absorb. If your book is set in an actual town—Dodge City, as an example—obtain old photos and a map of the street layout. A good part of *The Kincaids* took place in the town of Guthrie, Oklahoma. The local historical society provided me with old maps, pioneer diaries, and reprints of newspapers from the era. From that, I was able to recreate Guthrie, beginning with the day it was settled, the day of the first great land rush. The characters in the book knew their town because it was real to me, the writer. Through research, it came alive in cold print.

Once you're home, display the maps and photos in your office or work space. Steep yourself in the sense of the place, how it looked and where the prominent landmarks were located. When you begin writing, select only those details that are relevant to a particular scene. Everything you've recorded cannot and should not be transmitted to the reader. You're not a tour guide, and padding a book for padding's sake soon becomes obvious. Further, you should never stuff a novel with details simply to show the extent of your research. A Western writer works within a tight time frame, and there's no room for self-indulgence. Use the material to set the scene or advance the plot. Then stop.

Certain things, of course, must be imagined. The amber glow of streetlamps and the shadows of dark alleyways. The smell of greasy spoon cafes, the aroma of horse droppings, the odor of garbage heaps and outhouses. Yet all these things and more exist in those old photos. A magnifying glass and a keen eye reveals a world of detail. The boardwalks and muddy streets, the false fronts on stores and the variety of business establishments in a town. The interior of a saloon or gaming parlor, the look of a dance hall or a whorehouse, not to mention the Soiled Doves themselves. Old photos are a window into the past.

Wilderness lore requires research of a different sort. A writer who also happens to be an outdoorsman has a decided advantage. He probably knows how to build a fire and select a campsite, perhaps something of hunting as well. But what about trapping beaver or navigating by the sun or identifying edible wild plants? There's a whole sphere of knowledge unique to the wilderness, and to man's survival in the wild. Seldom is such knowledge contained in a single book, or indexed under a specific subject. Instead, a writer must read a wide array of books that deal generally with wilderness lore. Further reading about Indians and mountain men and scouts will provide additional nuggets.

A week or so in the wilderness wouldn't hurt, either. I was fortunate to have been raised among the Cherokee and Osage tribes. As a boy, I often took off with my Indian friends, roaming the wilds for days at a time. We lived off the land, carrying little more than blanket, knife, and rifle. The lessons learned there have appeared in any number of books I've written. Today, there are hunting guides and horseback camping tours, even survival schools, where you can learn something of the wilderness. Or perhaps a do-it-yourself program, simply packing into the backcountry, appeals to your sense of adventure. The point, again, is that you should never attempt to fudge it. Unless you've thoroughly researched it, don't write about it.

Of course, the extent of on-the-spot research must be weighed in practical terms. Simple economics dictates that you shouldn't spend more on research than you could reasonably expect to earn on the project. With travel so costly these days, you might reach a point of writing merely to subsidize your research. One alternative is to write the proper State Historical Society and acquire the necessary material. Old maps and descriptions cribbed from nonfiction works might enable you to do an acceptable job of fudging a locale.

The better alternative would be to set your novels in a location close to home. The research could then be done by car, in your spare time, without exorbitant expenses. Later, when advances and royalties reach a higher level, you could consider expanding your writing horizons. In the meantime, there's nothing lost by sticking to your own neck of the woods. Every region of the West has stories waiting to be told.

Experts and Old Timers

One of the most important aspects of research involves searching out experts. As an example, you'll often learn more about firearms of the era by talking to a gun collector than you will be reading a library of books on the subject. Over the years, I've called on oil men, doctors, mine operators, lumberjacks, and countless museum curators. All of them eagerly contributed their time and their expertise to my project of the moment. None of them considered it an imposition, or resented the fact that I would profit by their knowledge. In fact, most people attach an aura of glamour to novelists and therefore feel complimented when asked to participate. Never hesitate to call a complete stranger and request assistance in his area of expertise. You'll invariably receive a warm reception, and full cooperation. People like to talk about their specialty.

Old Timers are another invaluable source. While their numbers continue to dwindle, there are a great many of them still around. The search is worth the effort, and you'll find they welcome the chance to relive the past. Their reminiscences often provide information and insights obtainable in no other way. An excellent illustration is the research phase that preceded writing *The Kincaids*. The latter third of the book took place in the Oklahoma oil fields of the early days, roughly 1920-1924. Nowhere in the literature of the oil industry was there an actual description of how the wells were drilled and the rigs operated. I began calling oil companies, requesting a search of their personnel records. I was looking for a retired driller who had lived through the era.

By the end of the day, I'd found my Old Timer. His name was Charlie Jordan, quite elderly now and in poor health. We spent two days together, reliving every aspect of times long gone. Charlie drew pictures of the old rigs and taught me step-by-step how they were operated. I filled a spiral notebook with personal stories and the sort of information never found in historical works. Sadly, by the time the novel was published, Charlie had passed away. His widow, Georgia, was my guest the night I received the Western Writers of America Golden Spur Award for *The Kincaids*. In my acceptance speech, I paid homage to Charlie Jordan, and credited his great contribution to the novel. Your work will benefit as well by taking the trouble to search out Old Timers. There's an authenticity to their remembrances that you'll find nowhere else.

The Land

In Western novels, the setting is often used to create a sense of mood. The plains and mountains, even the weather, can be fashioned into images that evoke distinct feelings in the reader. To illustrate, either the stifling heat of the Southern Plains or the bone-chilling cold of a winter blizzard can be presented in such a way as to create a mood of suspense. The torrential spring rains that flood rivers and imperil cowhands on cattle drives can produce an element of excitement and danger. The serenity and quietude of mountainous high country can translate into inner harmony and a oneness with nature. All of these may sound overused and abused, bordering on cliché. Yet writers with a command of words continue to employ them with telling dramatic impact. The trick, as ever, is to express it with originality.

A brief description of the land serves to establish the setting. Sometimes used to open a scene, the description can also take place following dialogue or an action sequence. However, beware of lengthy, overly lyrical paeans to the wonders of mountains and plains. A travelogue, while fascinating to the one who writes it, usually puts the reader to sleep. The key here is moderation, bits and pieces strategically planted throughout the book. Let the majesty of the Western landscape overwhelm the reader gradually. Odes to nature are better left to poets.

Elmer Kelton provides a workmanlike example in *The Good Old Boys*. The protagonist, Hewey Calloway, pauses to reflect on the landscape of West Texas. Through his eyes, the reader forms a mental image of the countryside.

> *Until recent years this gently rolling rangeland had been a haven for massive herds of buffalo driven south each fall and winter by the chill winds howling across the high and open plains. They could find shelter here in the scattered stands of mesquite which fringed the wide draws and wet-weather creeks, and on the lee sides of the little bluffs and breaks which marked the southern-most fringe of the great caprock.*

Here's how I opened a scene in *A Distai   Land*. The description was used to establish a setting, the Hondo Valley in New Mexico. Later in the scene the valley was described in greater detail. The purpose here was to provide the reader with a sense of place.

> *A wind mourned through the leaves of the cottonwoods. Hazy sunlight rippled across the waters of the Rio Hondo, warm-*

ing the valley. Umber grasslands, like a wave crashing against a wall of stone, swelled toward the distant mountains.

Background and Details

Background must be tailored to fit the scene, for it is meant to evoke images that will enliven the moment. After writing four or five Westerns, I came to dread scenes which took place in saloons. Having described the typical saloon countless times, there seemed nothing left to say that had about it even a spark of originality. Yet I realized that the look and feel of a saloon enhanced the mood of the scene. So now, after thirty-one books, I still labor to create a sharp mental image of a particular saloon. Otherwise, in the reader's mind, the characters would appear onstage against a colorless, lifeless backdrop. Credibility demands something more.

Set piece scenes can also evoke a sense of mood. A device that never seems to wear on readers is the description of a room and its furnishings. In any home, the main room in particular (often called the parlor) tells much about the people who live there. Whether you introduce the people and the room at the same time, or bring the characters onstage immediately following the description, does little to change the effect. A lavishly appointed room, or one as spartan as a monk's cell, can be worked to create a variety of moods. Saloons, bordellos, and hurdy-gurdy dance halls all fall into the same category. The background provides scenery that can be shifted around any way you choose. How you describe it is what sets the mood.

Details are the sinew of a Western. They provide the fiber that holds the book together, adding strength through authenticity. Yet erroneous or misplaced details will live on to haunt a writer throughout his career. Western buffs, and that includes most readers of Westerns, are well informed on the era. One miscue might be shrugged off. A major mistake, even a few minor mistakes, will cause the reader to wonder if anything in the book can be accepted as authentic. The writer who neglects to check those small details will inevitably undermine his credibility with readers. The list of Western minutiae is endless: guns and saddle gear, foodstuffs and clothing, coal oil lamps and currency. Nothing can be taken for granted, or the writer risks a glaring anachronism. That's a three-dollar word for an historical gaffe.

Lack of research destroys what might otherwise be an excellent story. I recently read a novel set in Texas during the 1920s. The author had performed excellent research for the period. In the book, the 1920s came alive with his portrayal of living conditions, the advent of radio, and the growing reliance on automobiles. But interspersed throughout the book were flashbacks into the Old West. Apparently the author simply couldn't be bothered to do the necessary research. As an example, the Comanches were located in a section of the West they had never inhabited. To compound his error, the author had them still raiding Texas settlers long after they had been forced onto the reservation. Then, somewhat incredibly, he used the names of towns that were not on the Staked Plains until years later. The author's lackadaisical attitude toward research indicated as well a certain contempt for his readers. I closed the book midway through and tossed it into the trash.

Where to Start

Invest the time to uncover the details that lend flavor and authenticity to your novel. All the research materials you need are to be found in one repository or another. How do you identify nonfiction works relevant to the concept and story? Start with the history books you have on hand in your own library. When researching, save time and avoid reading an entire book hunting for stray pieces of information. Instead, consult the index at the rear of the book, where historical figures, events, and subjects are noted in alphabetical order. The meaningful passages are thus isolated and thereby speed your search. At the same time, check the bibliography at the rear of the book. Listed there are the historical texts and periodicals which the author used in his own research. Any number of these sources will prove relevant to your project.

The next stop is your local public library. Start with the card catalog files, which are usually categorized by author and subject. Then cross-check the bibliography list you compiled at home against the index files. Finally, talk with the librarian, who can often put you onto hidden sources of information. In fact, you should develop a cordial working relationship with your librarian. You'll find that librarians enjoy assisting authors, and their knowledge of research sources often proves invaluable. Moreover, they provide access to the interlibrary loan system, which extends to libraries throughout your own state as well as surrounding states. With your librarian's help, you can track down nonfiction works that have long been out of print. You'll be amazed by what a friendly librarian can uncover.

How to Dig It Out

State historical societies are indispensable to a writer of Westerns. Usually located in the state capital, a historical society is a repository of diverse information on people and events. There you will find virtually everything ever written, both published and unpublished, about the state in question. Old territorial maps, pioneer journals, business and political records, anything you might imagine will be placed at your disposal. If possible, you should actually go there and perform the research yourself. Often as not, what you stumble across proves more valuable than what you came seeking.

The alternative is to write a letter outlining the specifics of your research needs. Don't be vague; advise the research librarian, point by point, of the information necessary to your project. Request that the material be photocopied, and offer to pay for the service. Historical societies are accustomed to working with out-of-state writers, and their research assistants are trained professionals. Nowhere else will you find such a wealth of detail.

Various city and county archives are another invaluable source. Extensive records are kept, sometimes stored in their original form and sometimes transposed onto microfilm. Depending on your needs, you might check with the tax assessor, the county clerk, or the sherriff's office. City directories and court records, often dating back more than a hundred years, disclose incredible amounts of detail. As an example, the 1874 court records of Wichita, Kansas, reveal that Bessie Earp, sister-in-law of Wyatt Earp, was arrested and fined for prostitution. Further, the records establish that, during Earp's days in the Kansas cowtowns, he was something less than legend. In point of fact, he was an ordinary policeman in Wichita and a deputy city marshal in Dodge City. I worked all this into a novel entitled *Tombstone*. Yet, without the records, I would have never known. You have to search to find those nuggets.

The federal census also provides extraordinary detail. Taken every ten years, the census is organized by household and family members. The listing reveals who lived at a particular address, their relationship, race, occupation, age, and birthplace. Even in the wild and woolly West, nothing was sacrosanct from the census taker. Bat Masterson, who also inhabited the Kansas cowtowns, provides a case in point. The 1880 census reveals that William Bartholomew Masterson, then residing in Dodge City, was twenty-five years of age and living with one Annie Ladue, listed as a nineteen-year-old concubine. Later records, corroborated by the *Rocky Mountain Daily News*, reveal that Masterson skipped Denver with another man's wife and returned to Dodge City. Whatever else he was, Bat was apparently a helluva ladies' man.

Local newspapers are still another source for research. Their files are normally indexed by date and sometimes cross-indexed by name. These old newspapers provide a unique feel for the period. Advertisements for merchandise, articles on social affairs and politics, and editorials create a sense of time and place. Notable figures, whether railroad barons or outlaws, got wide press coverage. The material found in a newspaper morgue often provides the detail overlooked by historians. Old mail-order catalogs are equally revealing. Westerners called them "wish books," and they were read cover to cover. Among other things, these catalogs illustrate the clothing people wore, furniture, patent medicines, and a variety of everyday items common to the era. It's an archaeological dig in printed form.

Of course, an older generation of writers can draw on memory. Life out West in the 1930s was only marginally different from that in the 1880s. Hazing cattle or reading by the glow of a coal oil lamp had changed little in fifty years. I was fortunate to have been raised on a working ranch in Oklahoma during the late 1930s. Those memories serve me well when I write of people like my great-grandfather, who once survived a gunfight with three horse thieves. For a younger generation of writers, there are recorded recollections of pioneer cattlemen and homesteaders. Hundreds of such books exist, the majority published by university presses. Some of the most revealing, particularly about daily life in the West, are those recorded by frontier women. Their perspective of things was often more profound and insightful than that of the men. Nothing written provides a stronger sense of time and place.

Your Own Library

University presses are a major resource for the Western writer. Virtually every university publishes hard-to-find historical works in trade paperback format. These books are moderately priced, and it's possible to build a reference library without investing a great deal of money. Having your own books enables you to tab and underline points of information, rather than relying on copious notes or photocopies. Over a period of time you can put together an impressive reference library. I began actively collecting books in 1969, and today I have a personal library that exceeds four thousand volumes. As a result, I have at my fingertips material on any subject or time period relating to the Old West. For obscure material, I still rely on the interlibrary loan system and state historical societies. But the majority of my research can now be done simply by walking to the bookshelves. To start, compile a list of university presses through your local library. Then write each one and request that you be put on their mailing list. You'll shortly have the world of yesteryear delivered to your doorstep.

There's an added advantage to having your own reference library. Seldom is it possible to amass all the information needed before you start writing. Inevitably, points will surface that require further research. Certainty kindles creativity, and your novel will progress much more smoothly if you have the material readily available. Moreover, valuable bits of descriptive detail turn up while you're hunting for something else. These wisps of information lodge in your mind and later enrich the story during the actual writing. Digging for immediate research also uncovers plot ideas for future books. When you have the reference work at hand, you can tab the item and explore it at your leisure. In fact, your own reference library allows you to combine leisure reading with spur-of-the-moment inspiration. You'll trip across tales begging to be told.

Any discussion on research would be incomplete without a word about nonfiction writers. These scholars of the Old West devote their lives to expanding our knowledge of that bygone time. They receive little recognition for their efforts, particularly from those who profit most by their work. Every Western novelist should perform an annual pilgrimage to the Library of Congress and render an offering to historians. Without their dedication, novelists would never have access to the wealth of material available today. At the very least, we owe them a great debt of gratitude. Their historical works are the meat and potatoes of our novels, vital to any meaningful research. They deserve our admiration and our respect.

Historical Sources

Nonfiction is the raw timber of Western novels. Yet the beginning writer often has difficulty locating a cross-section of historical works regarding the Old West. Thousands of books have been published about the frontier era; to read all of them would require a lifetime. Here is a list of nonfiction suitable for general research as well as research on specific subjects. Some are still in print and others can be found only in libraries. Start by selecting those that relate to your current project. The balance should be read as time permits, thereby providing a broad overview of the Western experience. Novels of excellence evolve from a writer's devotion to research.

Across the Wide Missouri. Bernard DeVoto (1947)
American Indian. Oliver LaFarge (1956)
Apaches. James L. Haley (1981)
The Apaches. Donald E. Worcester (1979)
Arizona. Marshall Trimble (1977)
Bad Medicine & Good. Wilbur S. Nye (1962)
Badmen of the West. Robert Elman (1974)
The Bassett Women. Grace McClure (1985)
Breeds and Half-Breeds. Gordon Speck (1969)
Buffalo Hunters. Mari Sandoz (1954)
The Buffalo Hunters. William H. Leckie (1967)
Bury My Heart at Wounded Knee. Dee Brown (1970)
C. C. Slaughter. David J. Murrah (1981)
The Chisholm Trail. Wayne Gard (1954)
The Chisholm Trail. Don Worcester (1980)
Comanches. T. R. Fehrenbach (1974)
The Commerce of the Prairies. Josiah Gregg (1967)
Cowboy Culture. David Dary (1981)
Cowboys and Cattle Country. Don Ward (1961)
Crazy Horse. Mari Sandoz (1942)
The Crow Indians. Robert H. Lowie (1935)
Daughters of Joy, Sisters of Misery. Anne M. Butler (1985)
A Dictionary of the Old West. Peter Watts (1977)
The Earp Brothers of Tombstone. Frank Waters (1960)
Encyclopedia of Western Gunfighters. Bill O'Neal (1979)

Entrepreneurs of the Old West. David Dary (1986)

Firearms of the American West. Garavaglia and Worman (1985)

The Five Civilized Tribes. Grant Foreman (1934)

Frontier Justice. Wayne Gard (1949)

Gold Dust. Donald D. Jackson (1980)

Great American Cattle Trails. Harry Sinclair Drago (1955)

The Great Buffalo Hunt. Wayne Gard (1959)

Great Gunfighters of the Kansas Cowtowns. Miller and Snell (1963)

The Great Plains. Walter Prescott Webb (1931)

Heads, Hides & Horns. Larry Barsness (1985)

Hear That Lonesome Whistle Blow. Dee Brown (1977)

The Humor of the American Cowboy. Stan Hoig (1958)

The King Ranch. Tom Lea (1957)

Law West of Fort Smith. Glenn Shirley (1968)

Lone Star. T. R. Fehrenbach (1968)

The Look of the Old West. Foster Harris (1955)

A Majority of Scoundrels. Don Berry (1961)

Man on Horseback. Glenn R. Vernam (1972)

Joe Meek. Stanley Vestal (1980)

The Mystic Warriors of the Plains. Thomas E. Mails (1972)

The Oregon Trail. Francis Parkman (1949)

The Peace Chiefs of the Cheyennes. Stan Hoig (1980)

Phil Sheridan and His Army. Paul A. Hutton (1985)

Pioneer Women. Joanna L. Stratton (1981)

Prairie Trails & Cow Towns. Floyd B. Streeter (1963)

The Reader's Encyclopedia of the American West. Edited by Howard R. Lamar (1977)

The Red Man's West. Michael S. Kennedy (1965)

Saloons of the Old West. Richard Erdoes (1979)

The Shooters. Leon C. Metz (1976)

Son of the Morning Star. Evan S. Connell (1984)

The Steamboaters. Harry Sinclair Drago (1952)

Story of the Great American West. Reader's Digest (1977)

Sunlight and Storm. Alexander B. Adams (1977)

The Texas Rangers. Walter Prescott Webb (1957)

This Reckless Breed of Men. Robert G. Cleland (1963)

Time-Life Old West Series. Time-Life Books (1973)

Trails of the Iron Horse. Western Writers of America (1975)

A Treasury of Western Folklore. B. A. Botkin (1951)

War Cries on Horseback. Stephen Longstreet (1970)

The West That Was. Nellie Snyder Yost (1965)

Western Words. Ramon F. Adams (1944)

Winchester. Harold F. Williamson (1952)

Women and Men on the Overland Trail. John M. Faragher (1979)

Women Teachers on the Frontier. Polly W. Kaufman (1984)

The Working Cowboy's Manual. Fay E. Ward (1985)

Western Fiction

Your reading program should encompass a wide variety of Western novels. To be thoroughly grounded in the genre, you must expose yourself to the many different schools of writing. Here is a list that represents everything from high literature to skilled storytelling. The titles include traditional and historical novels, as well as generational sagas. For reasons of style and format, some of them won't interest you as a reader. You should nonetheless read all of them with an analytical attitude. Taken collectively, these novels provide a balanced overview of the Western field. You learn your craft by reading other craftsmen.

The Brave Cowboy. Edward Abbey (1956)

Windward West. Matt Braun (1987)

Rio Hondo. Matt Braun (1987)

The Trail to Ogallala. Benjamin Capps (1964)

The White Man's Road. Benjamin Capps (1969)

The Ox-Bow Incident. Walter Van Tilburg Clark (1940)

The Track of the Cat. Walter Van Tilburg Clark (1949)

The Snowblind Moon. John Byrne Cook (1984)

Aces and Eights. Loren D. Estleman (1981)

This Old Bill. Loren D. Estleman (1984)

Pemmican. Vardis Fisher (1956)

Mountain Man. Vardis Fisher (1965)

Wild Times. Brian Garfield (1978)

The Big Sky. A. B. Guthrie, Jr. (1947)

The Way West. A. B. Guthrie, Jr. (1949)

These Thousand Hills. A. B. Guthrie, Jr. (1956)

Warlock. Oakley Hall (1958)

Bugles in the Afternoon. Ernest Haycox (1944)

No Survivors. Will Henry (1950)

From Where the Sun Now Stands. Will Henry (1960)

I, Tom Horn. Will Henry (1975)

Carry the Wind. Terry C. Johnston (1982)

Gone the Dreams and Dancing. Douglas C. Jones (1984)

Season of Yellow Leaf. Douglas C. Jones (1985)

The Day the Cowboys Quit. Elmer Kelton (1971)

The Time It Never Rained. Elmer Kelton (1973)

Hondo. Louis L'Amour (1953)

The Wonderful Country. Tom Lea (1950)

The Searchers. Alan LeMay (1954)

Hombre. Elmore Leonard (1961)

Lord Grizzly. Frederick Manfred (1954)

Riders of Judgment. Frederick Manfred (1957)

Heart of the Country. Greg Matthews (1985)

Lonesome Dove. Larry McMurtry (1985)

True Grit. Charles Portis (1968)

The Sea of Grass. Conrad Richter (1937)

Ride the Wind. Lucia St. Clair Robson (1982)

Shane. Jack Schaefer (1949)

Monte Walsh. Jack Schaefer (1963)

The Untamed Breed. Gordon Shirreffs (1981)

Glorietta Pass. Gordon Shirreffs (1984)

They Came to Cordura. Glendon Swarthout (1958)

The Shootist. Glendon Swarthout (1975)

The Man Who Killed the Deer. Frank Waters (1942)

The Valiant Women. Jeanne Williams (1980)

Riders to Cibola. Norman Zollinger (1978)

PINE CR
CLEAR WATER
INYAN KAKA
BEAR BUTTE
Bear Cr.
BLACK HILLS
BOX ELDER
HARNEYS PEAK
SPRING C
RAPID
ELK
MAUVA
Porcupine Cr.
Porcupine Tail
HAT CR.
Wounded Knee
White Earth
IVER
FORK
HTNING CR.
OLD WOMANS FK
SAGO CR.
Guerilton
Bad Hand
Earth Lodge
Antelope
Rush Cr.
Dancers Hill
PHISTERER CANON
FT LARAMIE
R.
COURTHOUSE ROCK
CHIMNEY ROCK
FT MITCHELL
Cold Water
Blue Water
NE PASS
SCOTT'S BLUFF
PUMPKIN CR.
ERS
CHEYENNE
LARRONS CR.
ASH CR.
Russell
Julesb
Crow Cr.
FT SE
RADO
DEVILS SMOKE HOUSE
To Denver
SOUTH PLATTE
WHITE BLUFFS
Antelope

10.
How to Market
Your Novel

Writing a novel is the easy part. Getting it published can sometimes prove to be an ordeal. All the more so for a first-time novelist. So where do you start? How do you establish contact with an editor? How do you get your manuscript read? Luck plays a part in getting published, but far less than most people think. Hard work and determination are the critical factors.

You first need a realistic overview of the publishing industry. No one knows how many thousands of aspiring writers there are throughout America. What we do know is that every publisher receives dozens of unsolicited manuscripts every week. In the trade, these are called "over-the-transom" submissions, meaning manuscripts submitted by an unknown author rather than an agent. The volume alone makes publishers ambivalent toward such submissions. As you can imagine, the cost of reading all those manuscripts (to occasionally discover a writer) makes it an expensive proposition. Some publishers have simply stopped considering over-the-transom material.

Clearly, it becomes counterproductive for the beginning writer to send his manuscript out blind. What does work is to establish contact with an editor prior to the submission. In this instance, we're talking about a specific editor, the Western editor. Every publishing house has editors who are responsible for the various genre categories, mystery, science fiction, and so on. One source of editors' names is *Fiction Writer's Market*, published annually by Writer's Digest Books. Updated every year, this volume contains current market information, as well as a list of publishers interested in acquiring genre fiction. By consulting it, you know which editor to contact with regard to Westerns.

Another reference source is *Writer's Market*, also published by Writer's Digest Books. This volume presents a broad report on the publishing industry and provides excellent advice for freelance writers. You can perform a cross-check of your own by looking over the racks at bookstores and newsstands. There you will develop an immediate feel for who publishes what. Some publishers have an extensive list of Western fiction. Others limit their efforts to Adult Western series. Still others prefer historical sagas to traditional Westerns. What they publish provides a good indicator of what they're buying. You now have a list of prospective publishers for your novel.

Query Letters

For do-it-yourself marketing, the next step is a query letter. As the term implies, you're inquiring whether or not an editor would be interested in reading your manuscript. The letter should be short and businesslike, without any hyperbole about you or your work. Hold it to one page, with a brief description of the storyline and perhaps some mention of the principal characters. Conclude with an offer to forward the manuscript, and enclose a self-addressed, stamped envelope. Including the SASE usually ensures that you will get a prompt reply from the editor. Of course, there's nothing wrong with sending query letters to several editors at the same time. The likelihood that all of them would ask to see the manuscript is quite remote. Here's a sample of a typical query letter.

Dear Mr. Smith:

I have recently completed a traditional Western novel entitled El Paso. The story is based on an actual Old West lawman, Dallas Stoudenmire.

El Paso takes place during the summer of 1881. At the time, El Paso was the toughest bordertown on the frontier. No peace officer had been able to establish law and order in the community, even though several had tried. The town was controlled by gamblers and the rough element, and killings were a commonplace occurrence. An atmosphere of violence also existed between the Anglos of El Paso and the Mexicans on the opposite side of Rio Grande.

The town council hired Stoudenmire to bring the situation under control. A former Texas Ranger, Stoudenmire was a lawman-gunfighter with a deadly reputation. The primary story deals with how he tamed El Paso, killing several gunmen in the process. The subplots involve his troubled marriage and the racial strife along the border. The novel is fiction based on fact, true to the times.

The manuscript is approximately 75,000 words in length. The format lends itself to your current Western list, and I would be happy to forward <u>El Paso</u> for your consideration. Enclosed is a self-addressed, stamped envelope for your reply. I would appreciate a response at your earliest convenience.

Sincerely,

Businesslike and brief, this sample letter covers the essentials. First, the opening paragraph is designed to pique the editor's interest. Failing that, he might not read the balance of the query. Next, the second and third paragraphs quickly detail the primary story, the subplots, and something about the protagonist. The description is worded to indicate that *El Paso* is a traditional Western with unusual twists, an original approach to a standard plot. Finally, the last paragraph suggests that this novel would appeal to the publisher's current Western readership. That's an important point, for an editor succeeds by acquiring books that turn a profit. The enclosed SASE, and the closing line, ensure that the editor will reply within a reasonable time. Structure your own query letters along similar lines. *Sell* the editor on considering your manuscript.

Multiple Submissions

Let's assume two or three editors want to look at your novel. You now have the opportunity for simultaneous submission to several different publishers. In the trade, it's known as multiple submission, and publishers aren't fond of the idea. Time and effort may be expended in considering your book, only to discover that, in the meantime, you've sold it to a publisher who made a quicker offer. However, it should be noted that multiple submissions have never stopped an editor from buying a novel he considers worthwhile. From your standpoint, it boosts the odds of finding a receptive editor and saves an incredible amount of time. If you submit the manuscript one publisher at a time, and it's rejected, you could easily consume a year with three submissions. Take the route that works to your advantage. Go with multiple submission.

Never submit the original manuscript to any of the publishers. Instead, keep it in mint condition and use it to run off photocopies. To put the best face on it, find a photocopy shop that delivers high quality reproductions. Then, in your covering letter to the editor, state that you are enclosing a "copy" of the manuscript. There's no need to tell the editor that you've submitted copies to other publishers. The photocopy implies as much, and editors these days have become accustomed to multiple submission. If he likes the novel, it might prompt him to make an offer before another publisher does so. If he doesn't like it, then you've lost nothing in the process. The fact that he's reading a photocopy won't influence his decision one way or the other. A well-written novel sells itself.

Of course, it might not sell immediately. Editors are notoriously slow about considering the work of first-time novelists. Their work load is often staggering, and your manuscript might go to the bottom of a very high stack. If you haven't received a reply in sixty days, send a follow-up letter asking for a status report. If you haven't received a reply in ninety days, you can usually assume it's a lost cause. Which presents another good reason to retain the original manuscript. Failing a sale on the first go-around, start sending out more query letters. Order more photocopies of the manuscript and try to keep at least three submissions working at all times. Don't allow yourself to lose hope, and don't quit. Some of the world's great novels were rejected over and over again before finding a publisher. Your big break could come on the very next submission.

A word about manuscript format might be in order. First impressions do count, and editors equate neatness with professionalism. The cardinal rule here is no smudges, no sloppy corrections, and no crumpled pages. The format itself should follow a general standard, with all pages double-spaced. The title page should be a separate page, or cover page. Drop one-third of the way down, center the title, and type it in capital letters. Triple-space and type "by" centered under the title. Triple-space again, center your name, and type it in upper- and lowercase letters. On the first page of each chapter, drop one-third of the way down and type the chapter number as follows: CHAPTER ONE. Drop six spaces beneath that and begin the first paragraph of the chapter. On manuscript pages, the normal paragraph indentation is five spaces. The margins are usually 1¼ inches on all sides of a manuscript page. The page numbers should be centered ½ inch from the top, using -1- or some equally distinct style. Follow these guidelines and take the time to do it right. Your manuscript deserves a professional look.

You and Your Editor

Any discussion of manuscripts leads again to a discussion of editors. When you sell your first novel, you will enter a working relationship with your editor. Some writers hold their editors in high esteem and others roundly curse them. Over the course of sixteen years, I've dealt with nearly thirty editors. I found a few of them to be unimaginative drones, strictly nine-to-fivers working for a paycheck. The majority, by far, were concerned with quality and took a personal interest in my work. Several of them, after reading a completed manuscript, offered suggestions for revisions that vastly improved the end product. On occasion, some of them requested revisions that I felt would damage a particular novel. We discussed it in a reasonable manner, and in every instance, my opinion prevailed. Our working relationship endured because we approached it as one professional to another. I've yet to meet an editor who acted the part of a petty tyrant.

Copyeditors are an entirely different story. These are the people, often working on a freelance basis, who edit a manuscript for grammar, punctuation, and anything that looks drastically out of kilter. A personal aside will illustrate my experience with copyeditors. Following customary procedure, the editor returned the copyedited manuscript of *Hangman's Creek* for my review. Quickly enough, I discovered that the copyeditor had arbitrarily changed every line of dialogue in the book. It was now grammatically correct, but it was no longer a Western! I called the editor and informed him that his copyeditor had converted my Western into an Eastern. After explaining the problem, I told him to STET the entire manuscript. (STET is the proofreader's mark for "Restore to the original.") That particular publisher never again fiddled around with my dialogue. However, it's happened time and again at other publishing houses. Eastern copyeditors simply don't comprehend Western lingo.

The point here has to do with red pencils. The day may come when an editor, or a copyeditor, unilaterally rewrites portions of your novel.

When it happens, you'll be confronted with a major decision in your writing career. Do you stand your ground or do you opt to play the diplomat? If it's your first novel, tact may be your only recourse. However, after you've had a few books published, I advise you to defend what you believe to be right. Take that red pencil and mark STET in big, bold letters wherever it belongs. Otherwise you'll suffer a terminal case of heartburn through your dealings with copyeditors. Of course, when an editor *requests* revisions, you owe it to yourself to listen. The suggestions, more often than not, will improve your work. Whatever you do, adopt an attitude of professionalism. Nobody likes a temperamental author.

Nor do they like an ungrateful first-time novelist. With do-it-yourself marketing, you'll have no choice but to negotiate your own contract. Typically, the offer you receive from a publisher will involve a standard, boilerplate contract. The majority of publishers are reputable concerns operated by reputable people. However, business is business, and publishers always look to their own interests. Apart from the minimum advance and low royalties, you may be asked to sign over a large portion of the ancillary rights. To their regret, first-time novelists have later discovered that they assigned a major share of the movie and television rights.

Perhaps, like many beginning writers, you're willing to sign anything just to get the book published. On the other hand, maybe you know how to read fine print and you don't like what you read. At that point, you doff your author's cap and put on your negotiator's cap. Unless you know the game, you're liable to present demands that will sink the deal there and then. Or perhaps you're a skilled haggler and you'll wind up with a gold-plated contract. It could work either way.

Who Needs an Agent?

Let's consider the subject of literary agents. There's an old adage to the effect that an attorney who represents himself has a fool for a client. Something similar might be said about a writer who represents himself with publishers. On occasion, we hear about highly successful authors who act as their own agents. Yet a great author does not a great agent make.

Too often writers shortchange themselves by acting on insufficient information. A publishing house is a sort of hybrid money machine, with operational procedures unlike any other industry. Publishing contracts are intricate legal instruments, with interlocking clauses and convoluted language. The typical royalty statement conceals far more than it reveals, further limiting an author's knowledge of his own affairs. That lack of information can cost a writer more than he might imagine.

Here's a true-life example. The facts are correct, even though the names must remain privileged. A best-selling author was receiving six-figure advances on her novels. Her yearly income, including royalties, seemed to her a fortune. She handled her own business affairs, and she had an excellent relationship with her publisher. Then, through an interested party, she was persuaded that she needed a literary agent. A short while later, her new agent advised the publishing world that she was available to the highest bidder. Her old publisher ultimately won the bidding war by offering a $1,000,000 advance on each novel. She was both pleased and shocked, for she hadn't known until then the actual market value on her work. The agent further insisted that the publisher render detailed royalty statements rather than a simple accounting of monies owing. Today, the woman's annual income exceeds what many writers earn in a lifetime. The agent's 10 percent fee represents the best investment she ever made.

Writers too often focus on the 10 percent they're saving by not engaging an agent. Of course, some agents now charge a commission of 12-15 percent, and the saving appears even greater. What these writers don't realize is that their market value probably exceeds the terms they've negotiated for themselves. I know several Western writers who prefer to represent their own interests. A few get market value for their work; the majority are grossly underpaid. In addition, the time spent hawking books and hollering about royalty statements outweighs the commission they might have paid an agent. Worse, they miss out completely on lucrative deals that publishers will broker only through an agent. As for movie and television options, these writers are seldom even considered. They know less about Tinseltown than they do about the publishing industry.

What makes an agent worth 10 percent of your annual income? Well, first and foremost, he's an industry insider. He knows everyone who's anyone in the publishing world. His contacts have been nurtured over the years, and he's privy to insider information long before it's released to trade journals. Editors readily accept his phone calls, or an invitation to lunch, and they listen attentively whenever he pitches a deal. Conversely, editors frequently approach him with a proposition, some in-house concept for which they need a writer. An excellent example would be the Adult Western series, *Longarm*. At its inception, my agent received a call from the editor, asking if he could provide one or more writers. That same day he inquired as to my interest; I declined because I had no wish to write under a house name. However, I put him in touch with two friends, both Western writers, and they've each made a bundle through the years. The *Longarm* series is still going strong.

A good part of an agent's time is devoted to keeping abreast of the market. He knows what publishers are looking for at any given moment, and their requirements vary widely from house to house. His clients benefit from that knowledge by his ability to pick the right publisher for a particular project. One phone call enables him to kindle an editor's interest and submit a proposal for consideration. When it comes to negotiating contracts, his knowledge of market conditions plays a critical role. Getting top dollar is his primary goal, and he can often pit one publisher against another, thereby raising the stakes. Of course, in the end, a work of fiction must sell itself. An agent can open the right doors and put the project in front of the right people. Thereafter, a novel must stand on its own merit.

Any gathering of writers can stimulate a lively debate about literary agents. The most vocal are inevitably those who have a grievance. At one time or another they've engaged an agent, only to find that it did nothing to advance their careers. They view it as 10 percent down the drain, bitterly noting that the agent wouldn't return their phone calls, never got them a fantastic deal, and failed to propel them into the ranks of the literary superstars. What they never discuss is the fact that their novels are at best mediocre, and often unsalable. To admit it would require a degree of objectivity that few writers have about themselves. Their unimpressive record can more easily be dumped on the head of an agent. These writers choose to ignore the first rule of any commercial endeavor. A product, whether it's a novel or a widget, must compete in the marketplace. An agent can do many things, but he can't work miracles. He first has to have a salable product.

Contacts and Clout

Personal experience taught me how the literary marketplace works. In 1971, after completing three novels, I was in the early stages of starting a fourth book. Like many novice writers, I was acting as my own agent. I sent out query letters, submitted manuscripts to publishers, and filed away a steady stream of rejection notices. Then, in response to a submission, an editor took the time to offer encouragement. While she rejected the manuscript, her covering letter noted that I had raw talent and went on to suggest that I needed an agent. She included the name of an agent and stated that she had already called him on my behalf.

Three days later I met with the agent and he agreed to take me on as a client. After reviewing the first three novels I'd written, he told me they were unpublishable, flawed throughout. Under his guidance, I completed the fourth novel and began work on the fifth. Not quite a year later, he sold both books within the span of ten days. Today, some seventeen years later, we're still operating on a handshake. I credit him with getting top dollar for everything I've written. He's put together all manner of complicated deals involving packages of books, promotional guarantees from publishers, and several screenwriting projects. I spend my time writing while he negotiates contracts and delves into the murky world of royalty statements. The bottom line is that his 10 percent has been returned to me at least a thousandfold. By any measure, a helluva investment!

Perhaps you're unconvinced. If that's the case, I wish you well and hope you enjoy haggling as much as you do writing. For those who are convinced, I regret to say you've got a problem. Publishers prefer to deal with agents rather than unknown authors. Yet a top-notch agent will seldom take on an unpublished writer as a client. I'm not talking about agents who advertise reading services and charge a fee to evaluate your work. As you may have discovered, such offers rarely advance a writer's career. Nor am I talking about agents who operate out of a spare bedroom and depend on an occasional sale to make the car payment. I'm talking about agents with contacts and clout, the pros who wheel and deal within the publishing industry on a daily basis. Where do you find such agents, and how do you get your foot in the door? How do you *sell* them on representing you?

Once again, I suggest you consult *Fiction Writer's Market* and *Writer's Market*. There you will find comprehensive listings of literary agencies, their fee structure, and what sort of books they handle. You will also get some indication as to whether or not an agent will consider taking on new clients. Those who do generally require submission of a complete or partial manuscript by which to judge your work. The way to start is with a query letter, briefly outlining your experience and your most current project. When you get a positive response, fire off what you consider to be your best work and await a reaction. Perhaps you'll connect the first time out, and the agent will sell your novel for a bundle. More than likely, you'll write several query letters and wait a good while before you finally connect. That's all part of the dues a writer pays to gain membership in the club. Stick with it and you'll eventually find an agent. A talented writer always does.

There is a faster way to open the door. Perhaps you already know an established author who works through a literary agent. If not, then you should plan to attend one of the regional writers' conferences sponsored by various universities. Develop your contacts and convince a published author that your work has merit. Having done so, ask him to write or call his agent on your behalf. You'll still have to submit your work for appraisal before the agent will take you on as a client. Nonetheless, a referral from an existing client ensures that the agent will give your novel special attention. Over the years, I have referred upwards of twenty unpublished writers to my agent. Not all became clients, but those who did ultimately saw their books in print. An introduction of this sort rarely fails to open the door. Use those contacts to your advantage.

Finally, let's consider one other scenario. Suppose your do-it-yourself marketing has resulted in an offer from a publisher. At that point, you can approach an agent with a sale in hand. You won't offend the publisher, for all publishers prefer to deal with an agent. What you will do is put a professional negotiator to work on your behalf. Even so, perhaps you're hesitant to pay a commission on a sale that's already clinched. In that event, you're being shortsighted rather than taking the long-range view. First, an agent will obtain the best contract possible, usually far better than you would have gotten on your own. Moreover, you will now have an agent to negotiate your next contract and all the contracts thereafter. That alone makes it worthwhile to present him with the commission on your first book. Don't wait until the second book and keep the commission on the initial contract for yourself. Do it now, while you have a ready-made deal to open the door. You'll profit in the long run.

The world of publishing can be likened to a high-stakes poker game. Agents and publishers are professional gamblers, seasoned players who know all the tricks of the trade. An unpublished writer who takes cards in such a game relies more on luck than on skill. So do yourself a favor and accept the best piece of advice I have to offer. Hustle like hell to find yourself a reliable, top-notch agent. Over the course of your career an agent will protect your interests while negotiating the best payday possible every trip out. After all, your payday is his payday, and therein lies the incentive. He has a vested interest in your success.

Nobody could ask for more.

Western Writers of America

A writer with talent will always get published. When that day rolls around, I urge you to join Western Writers of America. WWA is a professional organization, founded nearly thirty years ago. The membership is composed of novelists, historians, short story writers, and screenwriters. Today, there are some three hundred members, split about evenly between full-time and part-time writers. The purpose of the organization is to perpetuate the tradition of Western literature in all its forms. In addition, WWA is a working organization, committed to furthering the interests of its members. Anyone who belongs would readily agree that his career has been enhanced by membership in WWA.

One of the major benefits is a monthly magazine entitled *Roundup*. Written and published by the members of WWA, *Roundup* contains book reviews, articles of historical interest, and vital market information with regard to Westerns. Of still greater import is the annual convention held by WWA. Apart from writers, those in attendance include a wide cross section of editors, publishers, and literary agents. Established authors, as well as newcomers, have an opportunity to meet one-on-one with a Who's Who of the publishing world. The convention program also includes daily seminars and workshops on various aspects of Western writing. The whole point of the convention is to assist writers in furthering their individual careers.

I joined WWA in 1972. The first novel I wrote was nominated for a Golden Spur Award, one of the many awards WWA presents at its annual convention for excellence in Western literature and film. I've also served on the board of directors of WWA, and the experience convinced me that membership particularly benefits the fledgling writer. For information on membership, write: Membership Chairman, Western Writers of America, Box 122, La Canada, California 91011.

A Hunger to Write

The Western novel, though rooted in another century, will never vanish. Man continually seeks new frontiers, but he nonetheless cherishes the old. We are a product of our forebears, those westering people who pushed onward in search of their destiny. So our national character evolves in large measure from our heritage, the realities and myths of our folklore. Our journey into the future will forever be lighted by our vision of the past.

The Old West was heroic beyond the imaginings of any novelist. Within the truth of that epic time lies the grist of our fictional tales. Your obligation as a writer is to portray it with honesty and rigor, without guile. Tell it the way it was and you will have told a helluva story. A story that will endure.

One final thought on our craft. There is a hunger at the bottom of all writing. Prestige and recognition, and a sense of personal accomplishment, are among the many rewards a writer one day hopes to attain. Yet there is something deeper and far more compelling that drives an individual to sit alone at a typewriter and fill blank pages with words. The compulsion stems from a motivation stronger than money or literary achievement or respect of peers. Simply stated, a writer hungers to write. He *must* write, for his hunger feeds on itself. All else is subordinate.

Anyone who doesn't understand that should seek another line of work. Those who do understand it require no further explanation. The hunger is there.

Write your novel. Write it with skill and precision and hunger. Write it today.

You'll never find a better time to start.

Index

About the Author

Matt Braun was born in Oklahoma from a long line of ranchers. At one time or another he has lived in Oklahoma, Texas, Arizona, California, Kansas, and Colorado. Having spent a good deal of his boyhood on a working ranch, he writes from experience. He is a fourth-generation Westerner, steeped in the tradition and lore of the frontier era. His books reflect a heritage rich with the truth of that bygone time.

During his youth Braun was raised among the Cherokee and Osage tribes. He learned their traditions and hunted with them, and along the way he developed an abiding respect for all Indians. Their philosophy regarding the right of each man to walk his own path became the foundation of Braun's own beliefs. Coincidentally, a branch of Braun's family played a distinguished role in the history of the Cherokee Nation. James Adair, a distant ancestor, wrote the definitive work on the Five Civilized Tribes. The book, entitled *The History of the American Indians*, was published in London in 1775. A year later Braun's ancestor married into the Cherokee Tribe.

Braun's great-grandfather founded a ranch in western Oklahoma and once survived a shootout with three horse thieves. Still another ancestor was one of the foremost ranchers in Texas. John Adair, a landed Irish aristocrat from County Donegal, came to America seeking investment opportunities. In 1876, Adair went into partnership with Charles Goodnight and founded the JA Ranch. Goodnight was already a legendary cattleman, having blazed the Goodnight-Loving Trail from Texas to Wyoming. With Adair's business acumen and Goodnight's cow savvy, the outfit was established in Palo Duro Canyon, deep in the Texas Panhandle. By 1880, the partners controlled one million acres of land and more than 100,000 cows wore the JA brand.

To a great extent, Braun is a man born out of his time. Like his ancestors, he has spent the majority of his life wandering the mountains and plains of the West. He has always felt more comfortable in a wilderness setting, and his books display a remarkable understanding of frontiersmen. He writes of a West where a hardy breed of individualists challenged and conquered a raw and hostile land. His heritage, as well as his contribution to Western literature, resulted in his appointment by the Governor of Oklahoma as a Territorial Marshal. Since 1972, when his first book was published, he has written thirty-one novels and three nonfiction books.

Among other honors, Braun won the Western Writers of America Golden Spur Award for *The Kincaids*. His novels are written with a passion for historical authenticity and realism, and based on actual incidents. Dee Brown, author of *Bury My Heart at Wounded Knee* recently commented: "Matt Braun has a genius for taking real characters out of the Old West and giving them flesh-and-blood immediacy."

Today, Braun lives in a remote section of mountains. He hunts at every opportunity, but like his Indian friends, he refuses to hunt anything he will not eat. He stays in shape chopping firewood, riding horses, and training on a boxer's speed bag. His weight is exactly the same (160 lbs.) as when he fought in the middleweight division of the Golden Gloves. Not unlike the characters in his books, he is a crack shot and works out consistently on a combat pistol course. He conducted survival training while serving a hitch in the army, and has written a widely acclaimed book on self-defense.